PRICE OF HONOR

THE BUREAU BOOK EIGHT

MICHAEL NEWTON

WOLFPACK PUBLISHING
— EST 2013 —

Published in the United States by Wolfpack Publishing

Wolfpack Publishing
6032 Wheat Penny Avenue
Las Vegas, NV 89122

wolfpackpublishing.com

Paperback ISBN 978-1-64119-561-4
Ebook ISBN 978-1-64119-560-7

To Tim Weiner (b. 1956)

DRAMATIS PERSONÆ

Colby Gantt: a CIA agent

Hardy Gantt: Colby's son, a CIA agent

Devon Gantt: an FBI agent.

Wyman Gantt: Devon's son, an FBI agent.

Nolan O'Hara: an FBI agent.

Erin O'Hara: Nolan's daughter, an FBI agent

Fiona O'Hara: an attorney.

David Jordan: an attorney.

Dominic Giordano: a *mafioso.*

Angelo Giordano: Dom's brother, also a *mafioso.*

Payton Sawyer: an NYPD officer.

Stephen Barnes: a KGB sleeper agent living in America.

AUTHOR'S NOTE

The Bureau is a work of fiction, but real-life public figures, institutions and events often appear within its pages. Where that occurs, personal conversations and actions are the author's invention, except where drawn directly from reliable nonfiction sources. Timelines of historical events, likewise, may be rearranged, compressed or extended as required for dramatic effect. Anachronistic terms now sometimes deemed offensive, are used within these pages as they were applied during the years portrayed. Obsolete geographical names are used as they were normally applied during the years of 1974 to 1983 inclusive.

PRICE OF HONOR

CHAPTER 1

May Day didn't seem to have much impact anymore, either in the United States or in the Eastern Bloc controlled from Moscow. Still, as Devon Gantt sifted the files and memos on his desk, it brought to mind a revolutionary time before his birth, when his late father joined the Bureau and did everything within his power to prevent Red progress in America.

Today, if Aloysius Gantt had been alive and active with the FBI, he'd doubtless be engaged in hunting commies and black militants.

The days of COINTELPRO-BLACK HATE were behind him now, but Devon still pursued the same old targets that were marked for government disruption before Edgar Hoover's death two years ago. One of them, H. Rap Brown, was serving time but still chasing appeals. Most recently, Brown's lawyer had discovered that Judge Lansing Mitchell, who'd presided over one of Brown's trials in New Orleans, had told friends in 1968 that he was taking pains to stay in shape, to "get that nigger" when the chance arose.

That meant another round of motions, writs, and whatnot, trying to help Brown slip through the net of felony convictions he had woven for himself.

In San Francisco, after a hiatus late last year, the so-called "Zebra" murders had resumed, with members of a "Death Angels" Black Muslim offshoot killing random whites. Police officials in the Golden State couldn't agree on murder stats in that case, floating body counts that ranged from fifteen dead to seventy-three. So far, there had been six shootings on January 29th alone, with only two survivors. In April five more fell, including an heir to the Du Pont industrial empire. Aside from dead and wounded victims, Frisco's tourist industry had taken heavy hits. Who wanted to spend time and money in a city where you might be killed for simply being white?

A $30,000 reward had finally cracked the case—or part of it, at least. An employee at something called Black Self-Help Moving and Storage claimed that prize, telling police that he'd been present at some of the murders, including one police had overlooked, a homeless "John Doe" tortured and dismembered before he was dumped piecemeal into the bay. Cash and immunity from prosecution got police four names and home addresses, though it barely scratched the surface of the virulent Death Angels cult. This very day, police had jailed four suspects, charging all of them with murder and conspiracy. Black Muslim Mosque No. 26 was fronting legal fees for all of the accused except one triggerman who'd pled guilty as charged.

The Black Liberation Army kept taking hits from law

enforcement nationwide, most recently in Georgia, where several members of the Atlanta cell were jailed, one switching sides to serve as a prosecution witness against slayers of a Bronx transit policeman in 1973. Out west, L.A.'s US Organization, once so useful in fighting Black Panthers, had dissolved into chaos after founder Ron Karenga drew a prison term.

Elsewhere, the American Indian Movement continued agitation on South Dakota's Pine Ridge reservation, clashing with vigilantes from the aptly-named GOON: Guardians of the Oglala Nation. Their beef, so far ignored by mainstream media, was that the rez suffered a murder rate of fifty-seven persons per 100,000 yearly, while Detroit—headlined as America's "murder capital"—lost only twenty and the U.S. rate at large fell under ten. They were pissed about it, and Gantt couldn't blame them, but the hard truth was that white America couldn't care less.

Add to that fact the dismissal of criminal charges filed against AIM leaders Dennis Banks and Russell Means for their actions last year, in the Wounded Knee siege, and Devon expected more trouble from Indian Country. The only question in his mind was who would die, and when.

———

Birmingham, Alabama: June 5, 1974

NEWS OF POLITICS was wearing David Jordan down. His work at Legal Aid distracted him to some extent, but he couldn't turn on a radio or TV set without suffering through more news from Washington.

Dick Nixon seemed to think he was an amateur magician, able to distract America with talk of an energy crisis, imposing a 55-mph speed limit on U.S. highways and adding nearly four months to the run of daylight savings time. Meanwhile, he'd first refused to yield his Oval Office tapes under congressional subpoena, then agreed to "edited" releases in the interest of "national security." The Watergate Committee soon discovered 18½ minutes suspiciously erased from one tape, but a secretary took the heat for Nixon, claiming that she'd done it "accidentally."

A fool who swallowed that, Dave thought, would probably believe George Wallace in a wheelchair was a "changed man" from the days when he could strut.

After one of the worst racist campaigns in Alabama history, Wallace had crushed four rivals in the Democratic primary and appeared to be unstoppable come November. It might've saddened Dave, but he knew how things worked in 'Bama and that knowledge made him wonder why he stayed.

The answer, naturally, was Fiona.

They had overcome the revelation of his family skeletons, which was a good thing, but somehow Dave kept waiting for the other shoe to drop. And when it did, he feared, it just might knock him flat.

————

LITTLE ITALY, Manhattan: July 15, 1974

"HOW MUCH THEY GET AWAY WITH?" Angelo Giordano asked his brother.

"Sixty grand, they say, so our cut's ten percent," Dominic said.

4

"The papers say it was a quarter mill."

"Whoever's hit always exaggerates," Dom said, "to make a profit off insurance."

"Are you sure about that?" Ange came back at him.

Their family had not participated in the payroll robbery, but since they'd licensed it, permitting a New Jersey gang to pull it on their turf, the 10-percent kickback was standard. What he *didn't* like was Ange suggesting that they'd gotten screwed.

"You wanna count it *fratellino*?"

"Nah. You say it's right, I take your word for it."

But he was skeptical, as any fool could plainly see.

Dom put an end to it, at least for now, saying, "You got my word."

The last thing that he needed was suspicion from his brother or loose talk going around the family. He thought about Chicago, where Sam Giancana had been hiding gambling returns from somewhere in the Middle East and stiffing the Outfit. Tony Accardo told a couple of his boys, "Explain the facts of life to him, and I mean *life*," but Giancana beat them to the punch and caught the redeye flight to Mexico, where he was hiding out.

More heat was brewing in Detroit, where Jimmy Hoffa had filed suit to scrub the part of his parole that barred him from a post in Teamster leadership for two more years. Hoffa's lawyers had slapped President Nixon's top mouthpiece, John Dean, with a subpoena in that case, Hoffa's unsubtle way of hinting that unless he got his way, he'd blow the whistle on their whole damned nest of thieves.

Dom wondered whether Jimmy had the balls to pull it off, and thinking that brought him around to worries on his home turf, with those crampy pains downstairs he thought might be an ulcer in the making.

Time to check the guns again, he thought. *Maybe tonight.*

———

Chicago FBI Field Office: August 9, 1974

THE OFFICE TALK was all about President Nixon's televised announcement from last night, telling the nation that he would resign "effective noon tomorrow." That meant any second now, with Vice President Gerald Ford of Warren Commission fame—appointed in December to succeed disgraced Spiro Agnew—would fill in for the Dickster until voters had a chance to validate him for a full term of his own or boot him in November.

While she dusted the glass doors of a LaSalle Street bank for fingerprints, hoping she could identify one of the morning's ski-masked robbers, Agent Erin O'Hara couldn't help smiling, recalling Lyndon Johnson's remark that Ford had played "too much football without a helmet," leaving him concussed and just plain stupid.

"What's so funny?" Agent Carl Mathias asked.

"Nothing," Erin replied. "Just happy in my work."

"Uh-huh."

One thing that *didn't* make her happy was creation of a new Senate Select Committee to Study Governmental Operations with Respect to Intelligence Activities, led by Idaho's Frank Church. Erin had no doubt they'd be dissecting the crimes of COINTELPRO, tarnishing the Bureau's reputation at the same time they were looking at the CIA, the NSA, and Vietnam. Not that Erin opposed a good housecleaning, but she had barely settled into her G-woman's role and she resented anyone who tried to spoil it for her.

On the good news side, she hadn't been a part of anything the Church Committee might be looking into, and she owed her new career to the collapse of Edgar Hoover's chauvinist regime. But would her father Nolan, on the job since 1946, likewise be spared?

Erin resolved to call him up tonight, where he and Erin's mother Keely lived in darkest Mississippi, and try to find out if she should brace herself for what was coming down the road.

———

CIA Headquarters: August 16, 1974

Colby Gantt was busy sorting files and shredding those that his superiors wished to conceal from Church Committee snoopers as the Senate inquisition gathered steam. It wouldn't help if someone started talking out of turn, but there were always ways to deal with that as well.

It helped that Langley had offloaded the responsibility for future U-2 spying flights onto the U.S. Air Force earlier this month, but there was still enough shit to be dealt with anywhere Gantt looked around the world.

Take the Vatican, for instance. Italy had revoked the Holy See's tax exemption from domestic investments in 1968, so the pope had hired international banker Michele "The Shark" Sindona as God's personal finance consultant. The problem: Sindona was tight with the Mafia at home and in the States, where he laundered the Gambino

Family's heroin profits. He was also a leader of the Masonic lodge called *Propaganda Due* or "P2," responsible for far-right terrorism in Europe. In January of this year, he'd been hailed as the "savior of the lira" and won endorsement as "Man of the Year" from U.S. Ambassador John Volpe in Rome. The ink was barely dry on that award when Sindona's Franklin National Bank went bust in New York, and now he faced indictments on two continents.

Of course, The Shark and P2 had been heavily involved in CIA shenanigans all over Europe and beyond.

Despite all that, Colby supposed the worst hotspot abroad was bound to be Latin America. Earlier this year, Congress had banned further expenditures to train and arm foreign police, thereby dissolving the Agency's Office of Public Safety. Many OPS duties had been shifted to the DEA and FBI, but the ban still slashed $150 million from Langley's yearly budget.

Not that it would help the citizens already victimized —imprisoned, tortured, slain—by military juntas and right-wing death squads in Argentina, Brazil, Bolivia, Chile, Paraguay or Uruguay. In Chile alone, at least 130,000 victims had been killed or "disappeared" by President Pinochet's goons in a so-called "Caravan of Death" roaming the countryside. One Pinochet opponent, former ambassador Orlando Letelier, had spent a year in prison prior to being exiled, then was traced to the U.S. and murdered with a car bomb in September, when he failed to desist from exposing the rape of his homeland. Meanwhile, "Operation Condor" spanned the continent, its goal "eliminating Marxist subversion" by any critics of right-wing dictatorships.

Stateside, one MKULTRA alumnus who wouldn't be talking was Charley Manson, transferred from Folsom

Prison to Vacaville's California Medical Facility based on "deterioration of his mental condition" in March.

Four hundred miles south of Manson's rubber room, in Los Angeles, authorities had charged another problem child, Joseph Merola, with fraud and stock manipulation, but Langley and the DEA teamed up to get him off the hook before he started blabbing, securing dismissal of charges against their "occasional source" of vital information.

Elsewhere, those who might have guilty knowledge of political assassinations dating back to Dallas kept dying, tongues stilled by the Grim Reaper. January's victim was Dave Yaras, a mobster who'd been tight with Momo Giancana, Jimmy Hoffa and Jack Ruby, gunned down in classic gangland style. February brought fiery death from an "accidental" stove explosion to Joseph Milteer, a Georgia Klansman who'd predicted JFK's murder two weeks in advance and later funneled cash to suspects in Dr. King's assassination. Finally, in August, lung cancer had silenced Clay Shaw while rendering moot his $5 million lawsuit against ex-D.A. Jim Garrison.

The worst potential problem, from an MKULTRA viewpoint, literally had gone up in smoke on May 17. The year had started badly for the Symbionese Liberation Army, with January's capture of members Joseph Remiro and Russell Little for killing Marcus Foster two months earlier. Retaliating for those busts in February, the SLA had kidnapped Berkeley sophomore Patricia Hearst, granddaughter of newspaper mogul William Randolph Hearst, demanding that her mega-wealthy family donate $70 worth of free food to every indigent Californian.

While that charade dragged on, the gang released an audiotape of Hearst—now calling herself "Tania" after

Che Guevara's former girlfriend—declaring herself an SLA member and pledging "death to the fascist insect that preys upon the life of the people." In April, bank security cameras caught Hearst front and center with SLA leader Donald DeFreeze in a San Francisco holdup that bagged $10,000 and left two persons wounded. From there, the gang moved to L.A. and robbed a sporting goods store on May 16th, while Hearst rode shotgun and peppered the street with bullets. One day later, an anonymous tip led LAPD and FBI agents to a house on East 54th Street and the rest, as someone said, was history.

Bullhorn demands for surrender brought gunfire instead, and the cops laid on with everything they had, from shotguns and assault rifles to teargas shells. Some bystanders insisted that a couple of G-men were also lobbying hand grenades. Two female members of the SLA emerged at last, shot by LAPD when they brandished pistols. One died on the lawn, while other members of the gang pulled the second back inside. Moments later, the house burst into flames, collapsing on itself as firefighters hung back in what they'd called "a let-burn situation."

When the ashes cooled sufficiently for cops to poke around inside, they'd found Donald DeFreeze in the crawlspace, an apparent gunshot suicide. With him, all toasted, were fugitives Camilla Hall, Angela Atwood, Willie Wolf, and Patricia Soltysik, surrounded by an arsenal of nineteen guns. The SLA had fired 4,000 rounds, against 5,000 fired by the police.

But where in hell was Patty Hearst? Nobody seemed to know, so she was added to the Bureau's Ten Most Wanted List, denounced on TV by Attorney General William Saxbe as a "common criminal" and "not a reluctant participant."

Gantt personally didn't care where she might be or what became of her. His problem with the SLA had been eliminated with the death of Don DeFreeze, a longtime subject of illicit drug experiments in California prisons, sponsored by the Agency.

Donald—alias "Cinque"—wouldn't be tattling on anyone unless they held a séance, and who'd even listen to him then?

————

HARLEM: September 12, 1974

NYPD SERGEANT PAYTON SAWYER wondered if he'd ever see the end of the Black Liberation Army. Despite its members being killed, arrested, jailed for life, regardless of announcements from his own police department that the outfit's back was broken, it appeared to take a licking and keep ticking like those Timex watches in the TV ads.

A case in point was JoAnne Chesimard, alias "Assata Shakur," who'd borne a daughter yesterday in a fortified psych ward at Elmhurst General Hospital in Queens. She had more felony charges pending than any other perp Sawyer could think of, but it never seemed to get her down. She'd been acquitted of kidnapping a Gotham drug dealer back in 1972, charges dismissed on a 1973 homicide, and the Jersey Turnpike shooting case had ended in a mistrial based upon her pregnancy. Two codefendants still faced trial in the New Jersey case, but the year's big BLA loser so far was Anthony Bottom, sentenced to life for killing a San Francisco policeman, backed up by twenty-five years to life for the 1971 Gotham murders of

Officers Waverly Jones and Joseph Piagentini if he ever made parole in California.

But how many from the BLA were still at large? he wondered. And what had he done during his years with BOSS to make them what they were today?

———

San Leandro, California: September 16, 1974

Wyman Gantt drove slowly down 139th Street past the bomb-scarred offices of Anaconda Corporation, an international copper mining empire owned and operated by the Rockefeller family since 1899. He knew his history, was well aware of all the crimes committed in the corporation's name against miners in the United States and South America, the union-busting and the firm's complicity in last year's toppling of Chile's democracy, replaced by an oppressive military junta.

He knew all that but was already drafting his report for FBI headquarters naming Weatherman Underground members he suspected of planting the bomb and issuing a flier that began: "We attack the Anaconda Corporation in international solidarity with the Chilean people and their revolutionary struggle."

It wasn't the year's first bombing, and Gantt knew it wouldn't be the last. March's target was the U.S. Department of Health, Education, and Welfare office in San Francisco, followed by a communiqué stating "the need for women to take control of daycare, healthcare, birth control and other aspects of women's daily lives." In May they'd hit the California Attorney General's office in response to the SLA shootout. June saw Gulf Oil's Pittsburgh headquarters blasted for its actions in Angola, Vietnam, and elsewhere. July's release of the Prairie Fire manifesto, 5,000 copies distributed free, spelled out the WU's goals and urged further revolutionary action nationwide.

Meanwhile, Gantt thought President Ford was aiding America's enemies, announcing a clemency program for 124,000 identified draft dodgers and military deserters, promising forgiveness without prison time in exchange for an oath of allegiance and two years' community service. What kind of shit was that, when Wyman and the other members of his family had risked their lives repeatedly to keep the country safe from enemies domestic and abroad?

Another goddamned sellout, he decided. Where was Nixon when they needed him, but off licking his wounds and playing golf with mobsters while he planned a second volume of his memoirs?

Christ, it was enough to make a patriot switch over to the other side.

VIENTIANE, *Laos: December 18, 1974*

HARDY GANTT HAD NEARLY MADE it home from Southeast Asia when the final U.S. troops withdrew, but then Langley decided there was still a chance to pull victory from a hat in Laos. Now he found himself lingering as the party did a fade, much like the Christians warned of nonbelievers being stranded when The Rapture came to Earth.

The good news: if his luck had truly soured, he'd be stuck in Nam right now.

In September, Congress had sashed aid to Nguyễn Văn Thiệu government from wartime levels to a paltry $700 million, much of which was siphoned off by Thiệu himself, leaving his army underfunded and dispirited. October saw Tôn Đức Thắng's northern government planning a major offensive for 1975, then they'd jumped the gun five days ago, breaking the Paris peace treaty with attacks in Phước Long Province. Today, Thắng and his military leaders were debating plans for final victory at Hanoi's Presidential Palace.

Things weren't looking good in Laos either, if the truth be told. With U.S. pullbacks, power had been shifting to the Pathet Lao while ailing Prime Minister Souvanna Phouma flew off to recuperate in France and declared plans to retire in early 1976, whichever way the war went. Effectively deprived of leadership, anticommunists staked their slim hopes on Prince Souphanouvong, the prime minister's abysmally corrupt brother, and his half-baked eighteen-point plan for "National Reconstruction." That impressed no one, and another nail was driven into Vientiane's casket when the Civil Aeronautics Board canceled Air America's operating authority in January, followed by closure of its base at Udorn, Thailand in June.

Which left Hardy with only one job to complete, serving as babysitter for the "Opium King" Khun Sa.

A Burmese native, born Zhang Qifu in 1934, Khun Sa had briefly served as a Buddhist novitiate, then switched to military pastimes and fought in the Chinese Civil War of 1949. Failing to crush the Reds there, he'd formed a "home guard" unit of his own in 1963, hunting Shan rebels for the Burmese government, financing his private army via opium. The Royal Lao army had bedeviled him for years, and turncoats in the capital at Naypyidaw had jailed him from 1969 to '73 on treason charges unrelated to drug-smuggling. He was only free today because his followers had snatched two Russian doctors from a Taunggyi hospital, swapping them for Khun Sa's release.

Today Khun Sa was the dominant opium warlord of Asia's "Golden Triangle," 367,000 square miles of prime opium-growing country centered on the confluence of the Mekong and Ruak Rivers, where the borders of Thailand, Laos, and Burma met. With 20,000 men, money and guns, Khun Sa furnished nearly half the heroin sold in New York City alone, rated 90 percent pure before Mob dealers started cutting it to boost their own profits. America's ambassador to Thailand had called Khun Sa "the worst enemy the world has," and the DEA had placed a $2 million price tag on his head, but Langley still supported him and was attempting to finagle passage to the States if he appeared to be in any danger.

Why not? Gantt asked himself. Dealing with drug lords was a time-honored tradition for global intelligence agencies, and why should he be any different?

———

FBI FIELD OFFICE, Manhattan: December 21, 1974

SPECIAL AGENT STEPHEN BARNES reread the transfer application he'd typed up in triplicate, checking the form for any spelling errors, then signed it and walked it to the secretary's desk outside the Assistant Director's office.

Barnes was applying for a posting to the Bureau's Counterintelligence Division and had noted fluency in Russian as a kicker if the boss decided to accept him.

Where better could a sleeper agent do more damage to the FBI from the inside?

Barnes hadn't minded working for the Criminal Division, even though he'd missed his shot at capturing a Top Ten fugitive eight months ago. A twenty-something punk named Larry Gene Cole, with his wife, had kidnapped a Virginia real estate agent in March and held her for $25,000 ransom, running north to shake manhunters off his trail. It hadn't worked: all three of them were found on April 3rd, the kidnappers busted without a shot fired outside Buffalo, 374 miles northwest of Gotham.

Barnes would've liked a piece of that, but what the hell? His mission called for more, much more, to honor the last wish of his late father in Moscow.

And Mother Russia still demanded his attention, even though he'd left it as an infant and would likely never set foot on its soil again. In February, onetime prisoner Aleksandr Solzhenitsyn had published his memoir, *The Gulag Archipelago*, and was promptly exiled to West Germany in lieu of being shot. In July Moscow had signed a treaty of friendship and cooperation with the Somali government, getting another toehold in Africa. Two months later, a council of military officers calling itself the *Derg* ("committee") had overthrown Ethiopian emperor Haile Selassie, and only yesterday announced the country would be socialistic from now on.

Sometimes Barnes felt as if he had been overlooked and left behind by history, but in those moments he remembered his blood father's burning passion, now his own, and vowed he would not fail the man who gave him life.

————

THOMAS CIRCLE, Washington, D.C.: December 24, 1974

AFTER NEARLY THREE decades of service to the FBI, Nolan O'Hara was fed up and bailing out. He hadn't made that step official yet, but with a formal resignation in his pocket, all he had to do was stop by Bureau headquarters and finalize the necessary paperwork.

That was one reason for his visit to the so-called Seat of Government today. The other was his covert meeting with a man who might make history with Nolan's help and that of other disaffected agents like himself.

An airport taxi dropped O'Hara at the downtown Washington Plaza Hotel, founded in 1843 and continually remodeled to keep its age from showing. Once inside the lobby, he used a courtesy phone to reach a seventh-floor room and confirm his arrival, then caught the elevator, listening to Muzak instrumental covers of popular songs from the Sixties until he stepped out on seven and followed arrows with directions to his destination. With 340 rooms to choose from, Nolan could've gone astray, but he was on a mission now and found the numbered door on his first try.

The man who opened it at Nolan's knock was short, maybe five-five, his head shaved in a bid to make a fashion statement out of going bald. He smiled, offered his hand in a firm grip that raised O'Hara's estimation of him slightly.

"Agent O'Hara," he declared, not asking. "I'm Paul Mueller. Thanks for meeting me."

"It won't be 'agent' for much longer," Nolan said. "My next stop after this is putting in retirement papers."

Mueller cocked his head and frowned. "No difficulties on the job, I hope?"

"Just the usual," O'Hara said. "I've done the same thing every day for half my life. It wears you down."

"I can imagine. Have a seat, please, anywhere you like."

Nolan sat on the couch, Mueller facing him from a wingchair. A tape recorder lay between them on the coffee table, with a microphone supported by a bipod that reminded Nolan of a sniper's rifle.

"Do you mind if I record this?" Mueller asked.

"Feel free."

After the tape was rolling, Mueller spoke his name, then Nolan's, with the time and date. That done, he said, "You understand we're hoping you might testify before the Church Committee?"

"That's why I'm here," Nolan confirmed. He had been following reporter Seymour Hersh's articles on the committee in the *New York Times,* paving the way for what was meant to be a free-wheeling investigation of the CIA, the FBI, and NSA, among other U.S. intelligence agencies.

"My hope—*our* hope—is that you may be able to supply details of Bureau operations carried out under the codename 'COINTELPRO' from your recollection of events during your tenure with the FBI."

Nolan considered standing up and walking out then, but he hadn't come this far simply to cut and run. He owed a full and public explanation to himself, his wife

Keely, and to his father's memory. He also owed it to his children: Ryan, no longer an agent since the Mississippi Klan wars turned him sour on it, and his daughter Erin, barely started out on her career. His testimony might make life inside the Bureau hard for her, but he'd discussed it with her in advance and she had urged him to proceed.

"I'm in," he told Mueller, "on one condition."

"Which would be...?"

"You tell the story warts and all, no coverups."

Mueller seemed to relax, smiling as he replied, "We wouldn't have it any other way."

CHAPTER 2

Chicago: July 14, 1975

Special Agent Wyman Gantt's belief that he would soon be separated from the Bureau's "Beards" had proven to be premature. Scanning the group of radicals assembled in a onetime warehouse on North Wells Street, at the eastern edge of Old Town, Gantt saw some familiar faces mixed with others that he didn't recognize. Two that he'd picked out from their FBI mugshots were members of the newish United Freedom Front, known for wounding a cop during a Portland, Maine bank holdup and bombing the Massachusetts State House.

Gantt knew he could drop a dime on them right now, but what would that get him? He'd likely blow his long-established cover and the pair might still escape, leaving the UFF founders and leaders—Raymond Luc Levasseur and Tom Manning, with their respective spouses—still in the wind and plotting revenge.

He preferred to mind his manners, taking mental notes on the attendees and guest speakers at this first convention of the Weatherman Underground's Prairie Fire Organizing Committee. Far from going out of business as he'd silently predicted to himself last year, the WU seemed to be going strong, even with several of its foremost members either jailed or on the run.

In January they'd bombed State Department headquarters in Washington and Oakland's office of the Defense Department, following those blasts with communiqués condemning America's continuing presence in South Vietnam. June's explosion rocked the Banco de Ponce in New York City, a flier announcing WU solidarity with striking Puerto Rican cement workers. Early July found WU organizers playing a crucial role in the Socialist Feminist Conference at Antioch College in Yellow Springs, Ohio.

Giving up? Not even close.

Although their politics repulsed Gantt and their rhetoric often struck him as pseudointellectual flimflam, he also felt a grudging sense of admiration for the terrorists who were the Bureau's mortal enemies.

At least they stood for something, even if they were wrong and verging on delusional. How many other people in his life could say the same?

———

Coney Island, Brooklyn: July 31, 1975

Riding on the Wonder Wheel, still going strong and

thrilling millions since its first spin back in 1920, Dominic Giordano slipped his right hand under Sofia Ricci's skirt and felt her thighs open a little, even as she said, "Not *here,* okay?"

"How 'bout here, then?" he asked and moved his fingers higher, pleased to find that she'd forgotten to include panties with her outfit.

"Jesus, Dom...won't everybody see us?"

"Let 'em," he replied. "That's half the fun."

In fact, their seat on the 150-foot amusement ride was just reaching the top of its parabola, and Dom surmised that no one down below, lights in their eyes, could see a damned thing that was happening atop the Wonder Wheel.

Distracted as he was, the slow circular ride gave Dom time to think about some of the recent changes in his world—which was the murky realm of *Cosa Nostra* in New York. Within the past six weeks, two heavy-hitters had gone down in flames, and that inevitably left Dom wondering who might be next.

On June 19th, shortly before he was supposed to testify before the Church Committee digging into Mob associations with the CIA, someone had killed Sam Giancana in the basement kitchen of his home in Oak Park, just west of Chicago. Sam was frying up peppers and sausage when the first shot drilled his skull, then the assassin rolled him over and pumped six more slugs into his face and neck. Cops claimed the shooter came in through a window, but they didn't have a clue who it might be. So far, the Chi-Town scuttlebutt was split between Tony Accardo and Florida's Santo Trafficante, possibly upset by Giancana's knowledge of the 1960s' plots to kill Fidel Castro.

But what about the CIA? Dom wondered, knowing that those spooks had just as much to lose as anybody else, if Giancana violated his *omertà* oath.

And then, just yesterday, who should drop off the Earth without a trace but Jimmy Hoffa from the Teamsters. Dom knew Hoffa had been fighting the provision of his sentence commutation that barred him from seeking any union office for another year. That threatened Frank Fitzsimmons's hold on the union, not to mention former president Dick Nixon's ties to Teamster money and the Syndicate. On top of that, Jimmy had also been subpoenaed by the Church Committee, someone likely realizing that he knew a ton of shit about the CIA and Castro, not to mention his blood feud with Jack and Bobby Kennedy.

So far, all anyone could say for sure was that Hoffa had made a lunch date with his fellow Teamster leader and cellmate Anthony Provenzano, longtime *capo* with the Genovese Family, now run by Frank Tieri. Yesterday, Hoffa and Tony Pro had scheduled lunch together at the Red Fox restaurant in Bloomfield Township, north of Detroit. Jimmy reached the meeting site at 2:00 p.m. and started getting antsy half an hour later, based on witness statements, when nobody else showed up. He'd phoned home then, telling his wife he'd been stood up—and that was all. His worried spouse had started making calls at 7:30, still no sign of Jimmy. Now the FBI was looking into it and getting nowhere fast.

The murders had no real impact on Dom or his small family, but it was still unsettling when the big boys started dropping. Hell, if they weren't safe, who was?

Something to think about, but it could wait until tomorrow. Now, Dom was busy with Sofia, looking forward to the party they'd be having when he got her off the Wonder Wheel.

———

FBI FIELD OFFICE, *Manhattan: August 2, 1975*

SPECIAL AGENT STEPHEN BARNES could barely keep from grinning as he walked back to his desk from the Assistant Director's office. His boss, John Malone, was retiring in a couple of weeks, but he'd taken time to summon Barnes and tell him that his transfer to the Bureau's Counterintelligence Division had come through.

As of tomorrow, Barnes was working on the Russia Desk—and one stride closer to his father's dream of bringing down the FBI.

Barnes knew he'd have to watch his step at first, couldn't risk making contact with the KGB too soon and setting off alarms that might betray him. Still, he felt that he was on the verge of something great, at last avenging the indignities his blood father had suffered at the Bureau's hands decades before Stephen was born.

Sadly, he'd missed his chance to personally ruin Edgar Hoover's reputation, though the U.S. Senate's Church Committee seemed intent on doing that work for him, albeit too late to shame and prosecute Hoover while he was still alive. And now, Clyde Tolson wouldn't see the next act of the drama either. Nearly crippled by a stroke in 1964, he'd suffered kidney failure during April of this year and died four days after admission to the ICU at Doctors Community Hospital in Maryland.

Ironically, the FBI's new headquarters in Washington

was nearly finished, scheduled to open next month as the J. Edgar Hoover Building. Barnes had made a weekend trip to see it, constructed on Pennsylvania Avenue at a cost of $126 million—more than twice the original cost estimate. It must be fate, Barnes thought, that even three years in the grave, Hoover was still bilking the government he'd claimed to love.

On foreign fronts, Barnes had been keeping up with news affecting Mother Russia and her reputation. In June, Portuguese interlopers had finally withdrawn from their longtime colonies of Angola and Mozambique, leaving both nations instantly engulfed in raging civil wars. Marxist governments had been installed in both nations, and Cuban troops were helping Angolan president Agostinho Neto crush opposition to his new regime.

Meanwhile, it seemed to Barnes that Moscow had been leaning over backwards to accommodate its erstwhile enemies in Washington. July had witnessed the first U.S.-Soviet joint flight in space, dubbed the Apollo-Soyuz Test Project, viewed by many pundits as bringing an end to the expensive "space race" launched with Sputnik 1 in 1957.

Then, in August, there'd been the Helsinki Accords, optimistically dubbed the "Final Act" of détente between the West and the Soviet Bloc. Signatories included Moscow, the U.S., Canada, the United Kingdom and every European nation save Albania and minuscule Andorra, tucked away in the eastern Pyrenees. For whatever it was worth, the treaty contained ten provisions, labeled The Decalogue by some unknown who'd clearly spent too much time reading the Bible. Those terms included: sovereign equality; abstention from the threat or use of force; inviolable borders; territorial integrity of all nations;

peaceful settlement of grievances; nonintervention in internal affairs of neighbors; respect for human rights and fundamental freedoms, including freedom of thought, conscience, religion or belief; equal rights and self-determination of all peoples; cooperation among states; and fulfillment in good faith of obligations under international law.

In short, the treaty promised grand Utopian conditions that had never existed on Earth and, from what Barnes knew of humankind, could never be achieved. It should be humorous, he thought, watching the various participants strive for those goals while failing all around.

And in the meantime, he had private work to do.

———

WASHINGTON, D.C.: August 17, 1975

NOLAN O'HARA WATCHED Senator Frank Church wrapping up his spiel on NBC's *Meet the Press* program. Church was targeting the National Security Agency without ever using its name, praising its high-tech spying capabilities abroad but warning of its danger to Americans at home.

"Now, that is necessary and important to the United States as we look abroad at enemies or potential enemies," he told the panel of reporters. "We must know, at the same time, that capability could be turned around on the American people, and no American would have any privacy left, such is the capability to monitor everything—telephone conversations, telegrams, it doesn't matter. If this government ever became a tyranny, if a dictator ever took charge in this country, the technological capacity could enable it to impose total tyranny, and there would be no way to fight back. I don't want to see this country ever go across the bridge. We must see to it that all agencies that possess this technology operate within the law and under proper supervision so that we never cross over that abyss from which there is no return."

"Damned straight," O'Hara muttered, wondering if government hadn't already crossed that bridge and leapt headlong into the dark abyss.

He switched the TV off and drained his can of Pabst Blue Ribbon, thinking of unfinished business that he'd left behind in Mississippi when he quit the FBI last year. Two weeks ago, a Louisiana jury had convicted Byron De La Beckwith of conspiracy to murder Jewish activist Adolf Botnick with a time bomb in 1973. Legal delays had stalled the trial, and various appeals would now ensue, making Nolan regret—not for the first time—that he'd helped save Beckwith's life on Tarawa more than three decades earlier, when they were both gung-ho marines.

In other Klan news from Louisiana, Vidalia Patrolman James Seale—a murderous Klansman linked to nine deaths spanning a decade—had busted a city judge for drunk driving and got him convicted. Meanwhile, a friend of Seale's, Robert Fuller—acknowledged slayer of at least six black men—had dissolved his offshoot Ku Klux faction, the Original Klan of America, when he was diagnosed with terminal cancer.

Nolan wished him luck with that: all bad. It still galled him to realize that he'd spent most of his Bureau career below the Mason-Dixon Line, investigating brutal racist murders in four states, and all he had to show for it was fringe participation in the "Mississippi Burning" case that saw seven Klansmen convicted of conspiracy. All seven were at liberty today, presumably enjoying life, a privilege they'd stolen from their victims.

At least O'Hara felt that he was doing something *now,* and if that meant going against the Bureau he had served for so long, as his father had before him, then so be it. Nolan didn't know if it was ever too late to speak out against injustice, but he hoped with all his heart that he had time.

————

FBI Headquarters: September 19, 1975

The U.S. Capitol stood less than a mile southwest of Devon Gantt's small office in the new J. Edgar Hoover Building, but it felt as if the two were worlds away from one another. In the Senate chamber, members of the Church Committee were reviewing decades of illegal actions by the FBI, the CIA and NSA, shaming the very agencies that kept them safe. Meanwhile, a short five-minute drive away, up Pennsylvania Avenue, Gantt and his fellow agents were engaged in last-ditch damage control.

The revelations about COINTELPRO, technically defunct for over four years now, were bad enough. But what would happen if the senators discovered all that hinky shit was still continuing, simply disguised by other coded names?

And why was that? Gantt asked himself. Oh, right. Because subversive groups and individuals kept plotting to destroy America, land of the free and launching pad for any crackpot with an axe to grind. If Bureau agents couldn't shadow and disrupt them, what did any of it mean? Why did the bleeding hearts in Washington even go through the pathetic farce of governing?

Black militants and their New Left accomplices had learned nothing from all the mayhem they'd engendered since the latter 1960s, but they had grown more adept at twisting laws to their advantage when they went to court. Take Rap Brown for example, now known as Imam Al-Amin. Exposure of the Bureau's COINTELPRO crimes, together with a comment from his white judge that he planned to "get that nigger," paved the way for an appeal that might spring Brown from prison.

More proof that some things never change: San Quentin had paroled Black Guerrilla Family member James "Doc" Holliday in July, after serving fifteen years on a murder rap, but now he was on his way back to prison, charged with two other ex-cons for a double killing during what LAPD called a drug rip-off.

Another one to watch, although he hadn't crossed the line yet, was Wesley Cook, aka Mumia Abu-Jamal, who'd left the Black Panther Party to become a self-styled journalist in 1970, serving as a de facto PR man for Philadelphia's MOVE Organization cult. Where that would lead him, Devon couldn't say, but any lawman worth his salt would want to keep an eye on Cook and his associates.

At least that wouldn't be a problem for the so-called "Zebra" killers in San Francisco, a fanatical Black Muslim spinoff calling themselves "Death Angels," earning "points" with their imam by killing random whites. A pal had sold them out last year, swapping testimony for immunity, and five of them were presently on trial for murder, the proceedings likely to continue past New Year's.

Elsewhere in California, ex-Bureau tool Ron Karenga

had qualified for parole and changed his given name to "Maulana" with the middle name "Ndabezitha"—"I've tried" in Swahili. He was still pushing Kwanzaa, the supposed African religion he'd dreamed up in 1966, and trying to resuscitate his old US Organization, once the mortal foe of Black Panthers, which had fallen into disarray while he was doing time.

Of course, it wasn't *only* blacks who set Gantt's teeth on edge. Two G-men, Special Agents Jack Coler and Ronald Williams, had been murdered in July, while pursuing an American Indian Movement fugitive on South Dakota's Pine Ridge Reservation. Violence had been rampant there for years, the unacknowledged death toll surpassing that of Detroit, America's current "murder capital," with tons of finger-pointing between AIM and GOON, the vigilante outfit run by tribal president Dick Wilson. Both sides had armed for war, with AIM emboldened by the acquittals of leaders Dennis Banks and Russell Means on conspiracy charges dating back to the Wounded Knee siege in '73, and now two agents had died in the crossfire. The double murder's prime suspect was AIM member Leonard Peltier, born on a North Dakota rez, now in the wind and posted to the Bureau's Ten Most Wanted list.

Meanwhile, another Top Tenner had been deleted from the roster two months before the Pine Ridge murders. Patty Hearst had kept on fighting for the SLA after her kidnappers-turned-mentors had been roasted in a shootout with LAPD seventeen months before. She'd helped build bombs the looney "army" used in two failed efforts to assassinate policemen, and she'd driven the getaway car from a California bank heist where SLA member Emily Harris killed an innocent customer.

Captured only yesterday in San Francisco, with SLA survivor Wendy Yoshimura, the newspaper heiress had listed her occupation as "urban guerilla" at booking and sent her attorney outside with a message: "Tell everybody that I'm smiling, that I feel free and strong and I send my greetings and love to all the sisters and brothers out there."

Gantt guessed that Hearst was angling for an insanity defense, claiming she'd been brainwashed by her captors, pleading major gaps in memory that dated from her kidnapping. One shrink had already described her as "a low-IQ, low-affect zombie," whatever that meant, and Devon frankly didn't give a damn, as long as she was taken off the streets.

It was too bad, he thought, that Uncle Sam didn't possess an island where such misfits could be dumped for good. And if the U.S. Navy felt like using it for target practice...well, who'd miss the cannon fodder, after all?

———

CIA Headquarters: September 23, 1975

COLBY GANTT WISHED he could get back to the field, somewhere away from Washington, but DCI William Colby wanted him close by, trying to minimize the damage caused by Church Committee snoops. Director Colby himself had been subpoenaed back in May, compelled to testify under oath despite pleas from President Ford and Secretary of State Kissinger that senators only "debrief" him on general topics, without substantive details.

And of course, that bid had failed.

Unwelcome revelations were a dime a dozen now, from the DEA's admission of employing fifty-three "former" Agency spooks, pulling the same dirty tricks they'd practiced for the defunct Office of Public Safety in Latin America, sending foreign cops for training at the FBI Academy, arming them through backdoor channels at the Defense Department.

All to what end? In June, when the DEA busted Tijuana Cartel boss Alberto Sicilia Falcon, they'd learned that his right-hand man, Jose Egozi, was a CIA protégé who'd been involved in the 1961 Bay of Pigs debacle, lately lining up mercenaries for a plot to topple the Portuguese government.

That news was still reverberating when relatives of Frank Olson, killed during an MKULTRA LSD experiment in 1953, won a $750,000 settlement from Washington, accompanied by half-hearted apologies from President Ford and DCI Colby.

Another shocker was the revelation of "Operation SHAMROCK," in which major telecommunications companies shared their traffic with the NSA from 1945 to the early 1970s, creating an epic "watch list" of presumed subversives. The Church Committee also found that DCI Allen Dulles had ordered Patrice Lumumba's murder in Africa fourteen years ago, but Agency killers failed to complete the contract before "others unknown" beat them to it.

South of the border, wherever you looked, Agency hitmen and their Latino confederates had been more efficient. Operation Condor had been racking up a score throughout South America, with present death tolls standing at some 30,000 in Argentina, 10,000 in Chile, 546 in Bolivia, 400 in Paraguay, and 215 in Uruguay. Those were the *documented* totals, borne out by official records, and stats were still coming in from Central America, with death squads operating in El Salvador, Guatemala, Honduras and Nicaragua.

Still, Gantt worried more about exposure in the States, particularly MKULTRA alumni like the remnants of Charles Manson's "family." One of Charley's girls, Lynette "Squeaky" Fromme, had served time for trying to dose a prosecution witness with LSD back in 1970, but then she'd rebounded in September of this year trying to assassinate President Ford in Sacramento, California. Supposedly, she sought to publicize a new group she had joined, called ATWA—for *A*ir, *T*rees, *W*ater, and *A*nimals—by shooting Ford point-blank with a .45 automatic, but in her drug-addled state she forgot to chamber a round before trying to fire it. Now she was in custody and facing a life sentence matching Manson's if convicted at her future trial.

The worst part of that mess was that *another* wacky woman tried to murder Ford in California, barely two weeks after Fromme's snafu. The second would-be killer was Sara Jane Moore, a forty-five-year-old West Virginia native, five times divorced with four kids, who'd served as a volunteer with William Randolph Hearst's food-give-away program after granddaughter Patty was kidnapped, while doubling as an FBI informer. Now rumors circulated that her fascination with the SLA might owe more to MKULTRA than simple obsession with weird news, but Gantt had it on good authority that any files containing mention of her had been vaporized at Langley.

Give her credit, though. Instead of botching it like Squeaky, with a stupid error, Moore had fired her .38 revolver at the president but didn't know the weapon's sights were misaligned. She'd missed Ford and wounded a bystander, trying to recover for a second shot when she was tackled and disarmed. Chalk up another life term for the loonies, while the Bureau tried to justify employing Moore as informer No. 04851-180.

At least, Gantt thought, before the Church Committee closed its inquisition, there'd be ample guilt to go around.

———————

PEORIA, *Illinois: October 30, 1975*

AGENT ERIN O'HARA double-checked her .38 revolver, knowing that its cylinder was fully loaded, but intent on making sure. She carried three speed loaders in her jacket pockets, hoping that she wouldn't need them, but she didn't ever want it said of her that she had died from lack of shooting back.

And these days, when the chips were down, she couldn't absolutely count on backup from her fellow special agents of the FBI.

A phone tip to Chicago's field office had brought O'Hara to Peoria, 167 miles southwest of her assigned office, traveling with five other agents—all men, which had come as no surprise. They'd staked out a motel on West Glen Avenue, waiting for Top Ten fugitive William Lewis Herron to show his face outside of Room 19.

A onetime used car salesman and bartender, Herron had been serving life for murder, robbery and burglary in a Kentucky prison when he broke out on August 15th, taking a hostage in the process. That added kidnapping onto his charge of unlawful flight to avoid confinement, and reports claimed he was packing two .38 pistols, one a revolver, the other an automatic equipped with a silencer.

There could be shooting, and while Erin had no doubt that she was up to it, she had to think about the other agents now and whether she could trust them when push came to shove.

Their beef with her, aside from basic chauvinism and resentment of a "girl" joining the manly FBI, was Erin's father Nolan. He'd retired from the Bureau last year, after twenty-eight years on the job, and before that he'd earned a Medal of Honor for his valor in the last World War. Predictably, however, all of that went out the window when he'd started working with the Senate's Church Committee to uncover past abuses perpetrated by the Bureau's outlaw COINTELPRO operations covering a quarter-century before Director Hoover's death.

That made her dad a "Judas" in the eyes of Bureau headquarters, and had fueled an ongoing campaign of snide remarks, cold stares, and unsigned notes left on her desk suggesting that she, too, might be a "rat."

They didn't seem to mind former Associate Director Mark Felt's role in toppling Richard Nixon with leaks to the *Washington Post*—some even admired him for that— and Felt had been neck-deep in COINTELPRO, keeping the faith in his recent Senate testimony about Hoover's missing blackmail files. "There's no serious problems if we lose some papers," he'd told the committee. "I didn't see anything wrong and I still don't."

They *did* bitch and moan about ex-Assistant Director Bill Sullivan's comments, partly payback for Hoover firing him abruptly in a petty snit four years ago. "Never once," he'd told the Senate, "did I hear anybody, including myself, raise the question, is this course of action which we have agreed upon lawful, is it legal, is it ethical or moral?"

Well, screw the macho bastards, Erin thought. She'd keep on playing for the team, and if the "boys" around her couldn't be professionals, they could go straight to hell.

The door to Room 19 opened, and there he was, one scumbag kidnapper and murderer as big as life. Something raised Herron's hackles and he bolted, sprinting toward his stolen car across the motel's parking lot.

Erin was waiting for him as the other agents from her raiding party shouted for their man to halt and raise his hands. O'Hara took the more direct approach, rising from where she'd crouched behind his vehicle and sighting down her Smith & Wesson's four-inch barrel at the target's startled face.

"Come on, asshole," she told him through clenched teeth. "Give me a reason. Pretty please?"

———

BIRMINGHAM, Alabama: November 10, 1975

IT WAS rare for Legal Aid to catch a headline-grabbing case, and David Jordan knew he likely wouldn't be in charge for long, but while he had this one, he meant to give it his best shot.

Which felt like it would be a major problem.

The defendant's name was William Turk, a black man who preferred the name "Sekou Kambui." He was twenty-seven and had joined in peaceful demonstrations until 1967, when he joined the Panthers in Chicago, then switched sides to the Black Liberation Army before heading south and founding his own Alabama Liberation Front. In January, cops in Birmingham had stopped him for a traffic violation and found a pistol in his car, reported stolen after a Klansman's murder in Tuscaloosa. Ballistics allegedly linked the same gun to a white Birmingham millionaire's murder soon after.

So far, it might seem cut and dried...but was it? Turk swore one of the arresting officers had told him, "We don't really give a damn whether you committed these crimes or not, but you *should have*, because we're gonna hang your ass with 'em anyway."

True or false?

It wouldn't be the strangest thing police in Birmingham had ever done, and prospective defense witnesses claimed they'd been terrorized by white cops to either recant or skip town. At least one had already vanished, and Dave had serious questions about the state's ballistics tests, which seemed to him muddled at best. Toss in cops grilling Turk about supposed liaisons with white women, together with a rabid press howling for blood, and Jordan hoped another lawyer would come forward to accept the case before it went further. If not...

When not neck-deep in legal cases, Dave kept track of Alabama's more notorious characters. Rabid Klansman Asa Carter had sold his pseudonymous novel to Hollywood, where international star Clint Eastwood was directing and starring in the film scheduled for a release next year. The trades claimed its budget was close to $4 million, with a fair chunk of that banked by Carter. Still, it wasn't all smooth sailing: screenwriter Philip Kaufman was on record calling the book's author " a crude fascist" and opining that "the man's hatred of government was insane."

Closer to home, Governor Wallace had announced his fourth run for president, coming up next year, despite many concerns for his health and stability after his shooting in '72. Fans claimed the media was picking on him with its footage of Wallace in his wheelchair, grumbling that if TV had existed in the Thirties, liberals would never have treated Franklin Roosevelt so shabbily.

Maybe not. But in Dave's mind, whatever kept Wallace from climbing up the ladder toward the White House was a good thing. Now, if Alabama could just find some way to ditch him as its governor, the state might be a better place.

———

CIA Headquarters: December 3, 1975

Hardy Gantt hadn't decided whether it was good to be back home again, or if he missed fieldwork in Southeast Asia. Most days, he supposed it was a bit of both.

In March the Reds had launched coordinated offensives in South Vietnam, Laos and Cambodia, scoring victories all around. Within two weeks, Khmer Rouge troops had captured Phnom Penh, and North Vietnamese regulars were drawing close to Saigon, where U.S. helicopters lifted out the last embassy staffers on April 29th. That same day, an Air America Douglas VC-47 bearing refugees from Vietnam had crashed at U-Tapao Royal Thai Navy Airfield southeast of Bangkok, all hands aboard surviving.

The fall of Laos took longer. Prime Minister Souvanna Phouma tried to spare his country further bloodshed by ordering his troops to stand down, apparently trusting half-brother Prince Souphanouvong—a Pathet Lao supporter from way back—to keep things mellow as the Reds assumed control. Yesterday morning, King Savang Vatthana had agreed to abdicate and the prime minister resigned, leaving Souphanouvong as president of a new Lao People's Democratic Republic. His first order of business: canceling future elections, consigning other members of his royal family to "reeducation camps," while launching all-out purges of the civil service, army and police.

So much for moderation.

Before all that happened, CIA case officer Jerry Daniels had evacuated as many friendlies as Air America could accommodate, including former Hmong guerillas whom the Pathet Lao threatened to "exterminate to the last root." Some 3,500 escaped, but tens of thousands more remained behind, presumably imprisoned or immediately executed by Red firing squads.

Looking back now at his time in Southeast Asia, Hardy wondered what—if anything—he had accomplished. When he'd had a drink or three, he grudgingly admitted to himself that while the Agency had helped forestall the bitter end, its efforts to resist the Red tide washing over Indochina had been a colossal waste of time and money.

By the time he poured his fourth drink, though, Gantt could admit that he'd enjoyed himself. It had been one hell of a ride, and he was looking forward to whatever turned up next.

HARLEM: December 20, 1975

. . .

THE YEAR WAS WINDING down and Payton Sawyer thought about the Christmas that awaited him. His parents were long gone, and Payton's sole surviving sibling was his sister Keisha, four years younger, who had finally divorced her cheating husband and seemed grateful when he took off for Chicago. Child support had been sporadic, but she didn't want to sue the bastard, so Payton had helped out with expenses for his only niece, Luvenia. Sadly, the girl seemed bent on replicating all her mother's dumb mistakes: no college, no prospects for meaningful employment, and a lousy taste in men.

To hell with it, thought Payton. He could just as well get by without a visit for the holidays, although he guessed Keisha would nag him into dropping by for what she called "soul food," poorly prepared.

Sawyer was coming up on twenty-five years with NYPD, most of it spent with "BOSS," fighting a daily war inside his mind while surveilling and subverting black "radical" groups. In essence, he'd relived his father's life— at least, until Ike switched from what became the FBI to serve with Bureau of Narcotics—but there was no argument that one group he'd pursued was radical and then some.

The Black Liberation Army had left a trail of blood from coast to coast, much of it spilled from cops the so-called revolutionaries killed or wounded. Payton thought it might be winding down now, but he'd thought the same before and been proved wrong.

In May, two BLA members awaiting trial at the Brooklyn House of Detention, held in lieu of six-figure bail, had tried to escape movie-style, knotting bedsheets together and descending that crude rope in a bid to escape their tenth-floor maximum security cells. One, Melvin Kearney, lost his grip and plunged 100 feet to his death on the pavement below. Another, Pedro Monges, made it down but hadn't cleared the jail's seven-foot fence before a rookie cop had spotted him and called for reinforcements.

Another BLA member, Richard Moore—aka "Dhoruba al-Mujahid bin Wahad"—was still serving twenty-five years to life for shooting two cops back in May 1971, but the U.S. Senate's Church Committee had given him new hope with its revelations of FBI COINTELPRO chicanery. Days earlier, he'd filed federal lawsuits against the Bureau and NYPD, alleging that both agencies had conspired to frame him by concealing exculpatory evidence. Payton knew that could go either way, but by the time various courts got through debating it, Moore likely would've served his quarter-century inside.

The wild card in the BLA's deck was JoAnne Chesimard, alias "Assata Shakur." Sawyer suspected she'd been slapped with more felony charges than any other single BLA member, with mixed results. So far, she'd been acquitted on a Queens bank robbery charge dating from July 1973, and in a Bronx holdup committed five months later. She survived a mistrial for alleged involvement in a New Jersey shootout that killed a state trooper and left her wounded in May 1973, legal maneuvers likely to postpone her retrial for another year or more. Most recently, just three days earlier, another jury had acquitted Chesimard of kidnapping a saloon proprietor for ransom in December 1972.

She seemed to have more lives than the proverbial cat,

but Sawyer reckoned something would stick to her sooner or later. And what would the BLA do then?

Not my problem, he decided. Payton had to get through Christmas first, and then decide if he had finally worn out his welcome at NYPD.

CHAPTER 3

ONE POLICE PLAZA, MANHATTAN: JANUARY 17, 1976

SERGEANT PAYTON SAWYER glowered at his desktop calculator. He had twenty-five years on the job so far, and nearly all of that with BOSS, but he was only forty-seven, still sixteen years out from NYPD's mandatory retirement age of sixty-three.

And how much longer could he take the bullshit he'd been wading through since he was twenty-one and trying to avoid conscription during the Korean War?

One thing he'd never expected to see was the Nation of Islam's dissolution, but the *New York Times* had covered it in black and white. "Prophet" Elijah Muhammad had kicked the bucket last February, leaving the sect to son Wallace Delaney Muhammad, who'd dropped the "Supreme Minister" title to become "Chief Imam" of a new maisntream Muslim group he called the World Community of Al-Islam in the West. Gone, at least in theory was the old mythology of Yakub "grafting" white demons from

45

original black men, and with it had gone demands for a separate black nation subsidized by Washington somewhere in the United States.

Whether the change would stick or not was anybody's guess, but on another front, the Black Panther Party was on its last legs, still reeling from the bloody East-West feud and militant defections to the rival Black Liberation Army. Huey Newton was hiding out in Cuba while a skeleton crew ran the national office in Oakland, but for Payton's money, it had one foot out the door.

That left the BLA standing alone, which was a lawman's nightmare in itself.

NYPD spokesmen might claim the group was dead or dying, but its soldiers in New York and nationwide still hadn't gotten the memo. Recent tabulations from the Fraternal Order of Police listed more than seventy violent incidents since the BLA surfaced in 1970, with thirteen dead cops on its scoreboard.

The BLA's lightning rod for trouble these days was JoAnne Chesimard, still battling various charges in court. Just yesterday, a jury in Queens had acquitted her of a 1971 bank heist. One teller ID'd her as part of the gang who'd pulled the job, but three others weren't sure and that was all the panel needed to release her, dismissing one security camera photo FBI agents had recovered—or perhaps doctored—to depict her in the bank, waving a gun. Two alleged accomplices on that raid had pled guilty but denied that Chesimard was with them when the shit went down.

She wasn't actually *free* of course. Another trial was still awaiting her in Jersey, for the 1973 turnpike shooting that left one state trooper and a BLA soldier dead, another gravely injured, and JoAnne wounded. BLA member

James Caston had died in the same battle, while cohort Clark Squire had received a life sentence for murder at a separate trial in '74. Chesimard has lost her bid for a change of venue to federal court, based on massive adverse publicity, and while she wouldn't face another jury till next year, her latest strategy appeared to be naming dead comrade Caston as the real cop-killer. She had a team of six lawyers on tap, led by radical mouthpiece Bill Kunstler, and for all Payton knew, they'd sell their version to the court. Sawyer already knew Chesimard's prints hadn't appeared on any of the murder weapons, nor could crime scene technicians find any trace of gunpowder residue on her person when she was booked into jail.

Not my problem, Payton thought, relieved—not for the first time—that he was a Gotham cop, not ducking bullets in the Garden State next-door.

God knew his job had ample risks attached to keep his nerves on edge, and he was glad he'd never married, passing that on to a wife and kids.

———

BIRMINGHAM, *Alabama: March 29, 1976*

"AN OSCAR NOMINATION? Are you frigging kidding me?"

Dave Jordan smiled at Fiona's reaction and tried to console her. "It's only for musical score, Fee."

"Who cares? The bastard shouldn't get *any* award for anything, unless they hand one out for being such a prick."

"Well, strictly speaking..."

47

"Yeah, I know. Some guy named Fielding wrote the score. So, what?"

"No need to make it personal."

"I don't believe I'm hearing this."

They sat together on Dave's couch, watching the Oscars ceremony broadcast from Dorothy Chandler Pavillion in Los Angeles. The film that had Fiona's knickers in a twist was called *The Outlaw Josey Wales,* adapted from the Western novel written by one Forrest Carter—better known in Alabama by his birthname Asa. Once a rabid leader of the Ku Klux Klan, he'd left the Cotton State after a failed campaign for governor and tried his hand at writing. He'd published his first Josey Wales book in 1972, followed up this year with a sequel and another tome titled *The Education of Little Tree,* advertised as a memoir of Carter's youth, being raised by mythical Cherokee grandparents coincidentally named "Wales."

That had been too much for the *New York Times,* which had exposed him as a former Klansman charged, but never tried, for shooting two of his own followers back in 1957. Carter denied his own name in the *Times* interview, but the secret was out now, perhaps embarrassing *Josey Wales* star-director Clint Eastwood.

Speaking of Carter, after his Klan faction bit the dust in 1957, he'd spent the next decade writing speeches for Alabama governors George and Lurleen Wallace, till he got pissed off at George for easing up a tad on racism and launched his own ill-fated gubernatorial campaign in 1970. That crushing defeat—placing last in a field of five candidates—had finally encouraged Ace to leave his native Alabama for the wide-open spaces of Texas.

To this day, Wallace denied knowing Carter. Of course, he'd also denied plans for another White House run in 1970, when he'd snagged a second term as governor, but that hadn't stopped him from running in '72 or again this year. He'd abandoned his fans with the American Independent Party, running in a handful of southern Democratic primaries, but only Mississippians turned out to pick him over former Georgia governor Jimmy Carter. Now Wallace had thrown his support behind Carter—an atypical southern liberal—but Jordan wouldn't put it past him to try for the Oval Office again in four years.

Meanwhile, a newcomer to Alabama politics—young Attorney General Bill Baxley—was shaking things up in Montgomery. This year, he'd reopened the Willie Edwards murder case from January 1957, charging four Klansmen who'd confessed to bombings during the bus boycott days but were acquitted despite their signed statements. One of the four turned on his fellow "knights" in exchange for immunity, but Judge Frank Embry had dismissed the charges, finding that "merely forcing a person to jump from a bridge does not naturally and probably lead to the death of such person."

Alabama justice.

Baxley had dropped the case, but rumor had it he was now investigating the deadly 1963 bombing of Birmingham's Sixteenth Street Baptist Church, hoping to make murder charges stick against members of Eastview Klavern 13. Dave wished him luck with that, but he'd lived through enough below the Mason-Dixon Line by now to know that decency and truth weren't necessarily enough to make the evil-doers pay.

And who was he to criticize, considering his mobbed-up relatives 960 miles away, in New York City? Just another Yankee prone to feelings of superiority that couldn't bear a close examination in the ruthless light of day.

———

Manhattan: April 24, 1976

Just when Special Agent Wyman Gantt thought that the New Left was dying from inertia and a shot of apathy, along came Congress to rehash the past and make it all look like the Bureau's fault.

Ex-Assistant Director Mark Felt had done his best before the Senate's Church Committee, acknowledging he'd ordered criminal activity against various radical groups, the outlaw actions rubber-stamped by ex-Director Patrick Gray. He'd gone on to say of the break-ins and other crimes he'd commissioned, "I think this is justified and I'd do it again tomorrow." Agents who'd committed felonies at his command were "just following orders"—the good old Nuremberg defense—adding, "To not take action against these people and know of a bombing in advance would simply be to stick your fingers in your ears and protect your eardrums when the explosion went off and then start the investigation."

And there were still bombers around, despite the Weatherman Underground's swift decline to around thirty members by FBI headquarters' estimate. The new terrorists called themselves the May 19th Communist Organization, dubbing their paramilitary branch the Resistance Conspiracy. Another was the so-called United Freedom Front, whose first attack, just yesterday, had been a bomb blast at

Boston's Suffolk County Courthouse. One of the bombers phoned a warning in ahead of time, but the explosion still injured twenty-two victims, one of them losing a leg.

Gantt's problem: heat from Congress had dissolved "The Beards" and officially ended the Bureau's New Left infiltration schemes. These days, an unfamiliar face stared back at Wyman from his bathroom mirror, and he had begun to wonder what was left of his career.

But in those moments, he could talk to cousin Hardy with the CIA and realize that little would be changed despite self-righteous posturing in Washington. America had enemies, and they weren't going anywhere unless a dedicated team of agents tracked them down and clapped them into prison cells.

———

FBI FIELD OFFICE, Manhattan: May 5, 1976

SPECIAL AGENT ERIN O'HARA kept her head down, focused on the file open before her, stolidly ignoring fellow agents as they passed her desk. She'd had enough of their accusatory glares and muttered insults since her father—now retired from service with the Bureau—had been featured as a Church Committee witness on TV.

So what, if some devotees of the old boy's network thought he'd sold the Bureau out by fessing up to crimes he'd seen committed in the guise of justice, unsubstantiated charges pressed while strong cases against the Klan and Mafia were filed away and forgotten. Most of her colleagues had started on the job when Edgar Hoover was alive and knew full well the felonies that he and his associates had ordered over time.

Now, thanks to Frank Church and his panel of investigators, all Americans who cared to know the truth would also understand that reign of error that had tarred the Bureau's name for nearly half a century—longer, in fact, since some of the illegal operations later tagged as "COINTEPRO" had begun with FBI attacks on labor unions and political dissenters prior to World War One. With Hoover in the driver's seat from 1924 to '72, longstanding practices were reinforced by the Director's racism and paranoia, foisted on the Bureau he had turned into a slavish cult of personality.

Still, many in the ranks revered him, wishing he were back in office to dispatch them in pursuit of Reds, "uppity" blacks, and anybody else who didn't fit the "100-percent American" mold.

What would her fellow agents think, O'Hara wondered, if they knew her dad had already agreed to aid the new House Select Committee on Assassinations, created this month to review the murders of President Kennedy and Dr. King? Somehow, the HSCA's marching orders had excluded reexamination of Robert Kennedy's assassination, only one month after King's, but perhaps the panel had enough on its plate as it stood.

Of one thing, Erin had no doubt: once word of her father' involvement with the HSCA leaked—revealing him as an advisor to the panel, not merely another witness—something rank was bound to hit the fan and blow her way.

CIA HEADQUARTERS: *June 15, 1976*

COLBY GANTT KNEW he should have expected changes at Langley, given the Church Committee's designation of the Agency as a "rogue elephant" responsible for countless crimes since its creation almost thirty years ago. Sworn testimony and surviving documents proved beyond doubt that agents had conducted operations banned by its charter on U.S. soil, while plotting the demise of foreign leaders, toppling whole governments, and generally acting like a branch of syndicated crime gone mad. He'd personally been involved in much of that and thanked his lucky stars that the committee's probe had barely scratched the surface.

Even so, the changes had begun four months before the panel's last report went public in April, summarizing outlaw actions by the CIA worldwide. In January, President Ford had appointed ex-congressman George Herbert Walker Bush as the Agency's eleventh director, heedless of the fact that he had no intelligence experience and that his father's bank had handled Nazi finances before Pearl Harbor. Three weeks later, Ford had signed Executive Order 11905, specifically forbidding CIA "executive action" against foreign heads of state. A new Senate Select Committee on Intelligence, created in March, now had responsibility for overseeing Langley and all other U.S. spying organizations to keep their feet on the mythical straight and narrow path toward lawful defense of America.

So far, DCI Bush's prescription for change consisted of the "Team A/Team B Exercise," in which a group of CIA analysts (Team A) competed with Team B's outsiders drawn from academia and a pool of military generals. Their goal: find out which group came closest to objective truth about a "National Intelligence Estimate on Soviet Strategic Objectives" as judged by—who, again?

Gantt didn't have a clue and frankly didn't give a damn. To him, it sounded like a steaming heap of busy-work designed to keep the media and Congress distracted while Langley went about business more or less as usual.

One troublesome matter dug up by the Church Committee was the subject of covert drug experiments both stateside and abroad. They'd come too close to home for Colby's taste, noting that under Operation MKDELTA "drugs were used primarily as an aid to interrogations," but adding that MKULTRA/MKDELTA potions "were also used for harassment, discrediting, or disabling purposes."

Not to mention satisfying George White's kinky sado-sexual proclivities.

Those revelations had prompted an addition to Executive Order 11905 requiring that "Foreign intelligence agencies shall not engage in experimentation with drugs on human subjects, except with the informed consent, in writing and witnessed by a disinterested third party, of each such human subject and in accordance with the guidelines issued by the National Commission for the Protection of Human Subjects for Biomedical and Behavioral Research."

That was fine going forward, but there were still mistakes from days gone by to be finessed and buried. Never mind the Manson family, with Charley locked in the Atascadero looney bin, his acolytes still jabbering nonsense as if their lives were just extended acid trips. Colby was worried more about the SLA, survivors of that weird experiment in terrorism still facing their days in open court.

Patty Hearst alone had been arraigned for the Hibernia Bank robbery, trial commencing on January 15th before Judge Oliver Carter. He ruled her "Tania" tape recorded statements issued as a fugitive to be both voluntary and admissible, along with a jailhouse tape in which she'd regaled visitors with a profanity-laced defense of the SLA's motives. On the flip side, Carter disallowed taped interviews between Hearst and defense psychiatrist Louis West, the judge sitting slumped at his podium, "resting his eyes" when West testified in person. Prosecution shrinks called Hearst "a rebel in search of a cause" and termed her role in the bank heist "an act of free will," further dubbing Hearst "amoral" and referring to what she'd called rape in captivity as "voluntary sex" with two SLA leaders, now both deceased. Judge Carter also allowed details of Patty's early sexual experiences, years before her kidnapping, and jurors had bought the whole package, convicting her of bank robbery and use of firearms in commission of a felony. Her sentence: thirty-five years in prison, reduced to seven by Judge William Orrick after Carter died before the formal sentencing date.

The court had never come within a country mile of linking SLA founder Donald DeFreeze with MKULTRA sessions while he was locked up in California. All that remained a secret, both from Hearst's legal defenders and the prying Church Committee.

Now, Langley had to keep its fingers crossed during another round of grilling by the House, this one designed to seek the truth regarding JFK in Dallas and the death of Martin Luther King in 1968. One troubling revelation came from witness Wally Weston, a friend of Jack Ruby's who'd seen Lee Oswald at Ruby's Carousel Club, plus Ruby's death row complaint that if that news leaked out, "they're going to find out about my trips to Cuba, my trips to New Orleans, all the guns and everything."

Granted, the Warren Commission had bent over backwards not to notice such pesky details, but with this new bunch in Congress...

On a happier note, potential opposition witnesses kept dying. So far this year, convenient heart attacks had killed Ralph Paul, a mobbed-up business partner of Ruby's; former Dallas motorcycle cop James Chaney, who'd claimed he saw JFK "struck in the face" by a bullet; and Dr. Charles Gregory, who'd patched up Governor Connally's wounds while the president lay dying in another operating room at Parkland Hospital. To that list, add William Harvey, CIA coordinator of the Agency-Mafia plots against Castro, deceased from "complications of heart surgery" in June, no further questions asked.

If it could only stay that way, with no more leaks and no one likely to confess spontaneously on the witness stand in Washington, Gantt thought they just might pull it off a second time.

If he was wrong, God help them all.

LITTLE ITALY, Manhattan: August 9, 1976

DOM GIORDANO DRAINED his third beer and immediately flagged the barmaid down to bring another. He imagined it would take at least three more to lubricate him to the point where he could finally relax.

The family he led was doing well enough these days, as far as he could tell. Their income from illegal gambling was more or less on track, despite a referendum by New Jersey voters that would legalize casinos in the Garden State. The law they'd passed restricted carpet joints like those found in Nevada to Atlantic City, but they wouldn't be completed for a while yet, and so what?

Atlantic City had been wide-open for gambling since Dom's childhood, only tamed a bit after the whole Kefauver inquisition of the Fifties, and it hadn't damaged Gotham's local play a bit. Real gamblers, the degenerates who kept the Mob in business, still bet through their bookies and their numbers bankers, come what may, and Dom knew the erection of a few resort hotels along the A.C. Boardwalk wouldn't alter that.

And drugs? Forget about it. Heroin kept pouring in, mostly from Southeast Asia, where the temporary end of wars throughout the Golden Triangle hadn't affected trade at all. On top of that, Dom figured that cocaine from South America would be the next big thing, likely supplied by a new outfit in Colombia that called itself the Medellin Cartel. He already had feelers out to tap that traffic and make sure he got a righteous share of it.

But cashing in, of course, meant Dom would have to stay alive and out of prison.

And thinking that brought two big Cosa Nostra names to mind, two made men who had climbed the ladder but had tumbled back again.

Anthony Giacalone from Motor City—"Tony Jack" to friend and fellow mafiosi—had been first to fall this year, convicted by the feds of income tax evasion back in June. No sooner did the gavel drop on that case, handing him ten years inside, when prosecutors followed up with further counts, loansharking and extortion, not to mention the ongoing search for Jimmy Hoffa. Tony Jack was one of two wise guys Hoffa was scheduled to meet for lunch the day he disappeared last summer, and the FBI was following that trail.

Still, ten years in the joint was better than what John Rosselli had received for dealing with the government. Two days ago, Miami fishermen had found his corpse, dismembered, jammed into an oil drum, floating off the coast. From what Dom heard, the hit had been occasioned by Rosselli's testimony to the Senate's Church Committee, spilling damn near everything he knew about the CIA and certain *mafiosi* teaming up to kill Fidel Castro back in the Sixties. There were also fears that he might have more stories—about JFK for instance—that would pique the interest of a new committee forming up in Washington, taking another look-see at the Dallas deal and Martin Luther King's murder in Memphis, once the preacher crossed Carlos Marcello by his meddling in the Memphis garbage rackets.

Add that hit to Momo Giancana's execution fourteen months ago, and Dom could read the message loud and clear without a Gypsy helping him. It was a serious mistake to deal with feds while hoping you'd get something out of it.

At least Dom's Uncle Primo and his father Carlo had avoided being snared in all that *merda*. Now, all Dominic had to consider was the DEA trying to make a reputation for itself by busting people like himself, who worked for their living.

His beer arrived, and Giordano tipped the waitress, telling her, "You'd better keep 'em coming, Babe. How long until last call?"

_____

Rock Creek Park, Washington, D.C.: September 25, 1976

NOLAN O'HARA LIKED to get away from home sometimes, be by himself and think about the course his life had taken since he'd left the Bureau. His wife Keely didn't seem to mind when Nolan talked about it, but he had a hunch some of the things he'd seen and done depressed her.

And he knew she worried about Nolan's choice of going up against the FBI.

Headquarters couldn't touch his pension, but there were so many other ways the government could mess with people—tax audits, compiling bullshit dossiers in case he ever tried to get another job or doling out derogatory information to discredit any public statements he might make—that Nolan understood why she might worry.

As for him, the only drawback he saw to unburdening himself was damage it might do to daughter Erin, four years on the job now, still assigned to the Chicago field office their father served during the old gangbuster days.

It had been risky, going public with the Church Committee, and now Nolan had this new gig with the House Select Committee on Assassinations. He'd heard stories about Dallas from his father and had done some snooping on his own through Bureau files that weren't restricted to eyes-only for the brass at headquarters. O'Hara knew the Bureau had concealed no end of information about contacts with Lee Oswald prior to November 1963, Jack Ruby's ties to syndicated crime, and

CIA chicanery conducted under euphemisms such as "executive action" against heads of state.

Now, he'd decided it was time to share that knowledge with America at large—or give the HSCA's staff pointers, at least—and let the chips fall where they may.

He'd met the new committee's chairman, Thomas Downing from Virginia, hand-picked by Speaker of the House Carl Albert to ride herd on the panel of nine fellow Democrats and four Republicans. The committee's chief counsel was Richard Sprague, a navy veteran and cofounder of California's Computer Research Corporation, who'd started probing the JFK murder on his own in 1966, after he'd seen the infamous Zapruder film for the first time. He'd served as a photographic expert for New Orleans D.A. Jim Garrison on the muddled Clay Shaw conspiracy trial and cofounded a Committee to Investigate Assassinations with lawyer Bernard Fensterwald, who'd defended both alleged assassin James Earl Ray and Watergate "plumber" James McCord—an odd couple if ever there was one.

So far, O'Hara thought that Downing and his people were sincere, unlike the Warren Commission's whitewash artists, the Bureau gremlins who'd buried tantalizing leads in Dr. King's assassination, and LAPD's part-time CIA agents who'd dropped the ball big-time on Bobby Kennedy's murder, one month after King's.

Sincerity was helpful, but O'Hara knew it couldn't always pierce the veil of bullshit raised by intelligence agencies any time they had something to hide.

The question now, as Nolan saw it, was twofold: How much material of any value still survived in various official files? And how would anyone unearth it when it had been buried for so many years?

———

FBI FIELD OFFICE, Manhattan: October 5, 1976

SPECIAL AGENT STEPHEN BARNES was on his way, had taken an irrevocable step toward selling out the FBI as planned decades before his birth by unacknowledged father Leonid Babin. He had made cautious contact with an agent of the KGB and was prepared to launch a long-term leak of classified material from Bureau files to Moscow, but he'd have to watch his step.

The stakes were huge, and one simple mistake could cost his freedom—or his life.

His contact had no ties to Russia's embassy in the United States or to Yakov Malik, Russia's present representative to the United Nations. After some determined sleuthing, aided by Stephen's adoptive parents, sleeper agents Mark and Isabella Barnes, he'd finally contacted Alexander Bobrik, holding the rank of *Podpolkovnik*—Lieutenant-Colonel—with the KGB's First Directorate, in charge of Foreign Operations.

Which, of course, meant spying overseas.

Connecting with the officer who'd be his Russian handler had started like a chess game played by mail. Stephen's adoptive parents had obtained a name from their handler and passed it on, with the address of a private mail drop on Times Square. A month before he ever met Bobrik in person, Barnes had risked a cryptic letter to the agent's post office box, including coded phrases fed to him by Mark and Isabella. His return address was yet another mail drop, situated in a storefront seven blocks from Bobrik's drop. The answer he'd received, after a week's delay, included questions that might pass for innocent, but which required inclusion of his badge and Social Security numbers inserted as seemingly random stock numbers for items Barnes wished to purchase.

From there, another two weeks passed, presumably while Bobrik used his network to confirm Stephen's identity, his field office assignment to Counterintelligence, and likely included some form of surveillance he hadn't detected. When they met at last, it was a Sunday afternoon, perfect for chance encounters on The Ramble—thirty-eight acres of woodland paths in Central Park, between 73rd and 78th Streets. Barnes had gone alone, while Bobrik brought a thug along with him to frisk Barnes, followed by a scan from head-to-toe with a device resembling a transistor radio, clearly designed to sniff out any microphones Barnes might have hidden on his person.

Once the muscle drifted off to let them speak in peace, Barnes had assessed his contact: fifty-something, five foot eight or nine, with graying brush cut hair that matched the color of his watchful eyes behind a pair of wire-rimmed spectacles. Bobrik refrained from smoking, but his casual attire carried aromas of tobacco that were unmistakable.

Their conversation had established rules for contact and the kinds of FBI material the KGB preferred—in short, whatever might pertain to Russia or her satellites, the nation's diplomats worldwide, and most particularly news about traitorous double agents or defectors. Barnes nearly laughed aloud when Bobrik offered payment of $1,200 per month, then caught himself and gratefully accepted.

Money was a motive that the KGB would understand, unlike a scheme hatched by his father long before Stephen—or Stefan, at the time—was born. Barnes had no reason to believe that current KGB Chairman Yuri Andropov knew anything about the dream of vengeance that had driven Leonid Babin for the better part of half a century, intent on bringing down the mighty FBI which had deported him not once, but twice.

Before they'd parted, Bobrik had supplied a tiny camera designed for photographing documents, instructed Barnes to process any negatives and prints himself, then gave Barnes the address of yet another mail drop, located on East 64th Street between Park and Madison Avenues. Barnes found his first attempt at photographing Bureau files to be a nerve-racking experience but got it done and mailed the processed negatives to Bobrik as required. Within three days, his new post office box received an envelope containing twelve crisp, new $100 bills.

So, Barnes was on his way, and all the while he kept close track of daily happenings around the Gotham field office, and from the world at large. The Church Committee's findings likely would have driven Edgar Hoover to a heart attack, if he'd been living when those revelations hit the media. In March, Attorney General Edward Levi hit the Bureau with guidelines for future intelligence activities, broadened in April to include domestic security actions. Congress had imposed a maximum ten-year term for future FBI directors, and only yesterday, headquarters had announced creation of a new Office of Professional Responsibility—the equivalent of a police department's Internal Affairs Division, tasked with investigating malfeasance complaints against Bureau agents.

In Asia, Mao Zedong had died last month, replaced by Hua Guofeng as sixth chairman of the Chinese Communist Party. Thus far, Chairman Hua had ended the chaotic Cultural Revolution, launched ten years earlier, and he was now pursuing treason charges against the "Gang of Four" that sought ultimate power after Mao's death. Those accused included Jiang Qing, aka "Madam Mao," a 1930s actress who had been Mao's fourth and final wife; second-ranked Vice Premier Zhang Chunqiao; second Vice-Chairman of the CCP Wang Hongwen; and Yao Wenyuan, a CCP Politburo member and editor of Shanghai's *Liberation Daily* newspaper.

Unless Barnes missed his guess, all four would soon be shot or locked away in prison cells. And when they were, there'd be more files for him to photograph and transmit to his KGB contact, another body blow against the mighty FBI.

———

FBI Headquarters: October 12, 1976

THE CHURCH COMMITTEE might have shoveled more dirt onto COINTELPRO's grave, but despite its seamy revelations, Special Agent Devon Gantt was still pursuing business more or less as usual. Director Clarence Kelley had to pay lip service to the Senate and Attorney General, mouthing platitudes that indicated he was "cleaning house," but no one from the Hoover days had been dismissed so far, and most of them—like Gantt—were still tracking the same subversives they'd pursued before the Old Man turned up dead four years ago.

Take "Black Hate," for example. Suitably chastised, the Bureau no longer applied that label to such groups as the late Dr. King's SCLC, but any militants who stepped across the line from prayers and nonviolent "We Shall Overcome" philosophy still wound up in the Bureau's files, and frequently in prison.

Rap Brown, aka "Imam Al-Amin," was a good case in point. Leftist attorneys led by Bill Kunstler had wangled Brown's parole after serving five years in New York, and they'd persuaded Justice to drop more charges pending against him in New Orleans. After receiving tons of letters from Brown's fans, the Bureau of Prisons allowed Rap to shift his parole from New York to Atlanta, where he'd settled in the city's West End and founded something called the Community Mosque of Atlanta.

Onetime FBI informer Ron Karenga, another ex-con on the move, had revived his US Organization and secured a Ph.D. from the L.A.-based United States International University for a 170-page dissertation titled "Afro-American Nationalism: Social Strategy and Struggle for Community." Gantt hadn't read the paper, but he assumed it had little to say about stalking Black Panthers.

The Black Guerrilla Family kept making headlines from prison. In January a federal judge deemed official treatment of the group's "San Quentin Six" cruel and unusual, ordering that they not be chained around the neck, waist and groin except during transport. At their trial in August, jurors convicted Hugo Pinell and David Johnson of assaulting prison guards but acquitted both of conspiracy, freeing Johnson on the basis of time served. The same panel convicted BGF member Johnny Spain of killing two guards during the 1971 riot that also claimed

George Jackson's life, but cleared him of slaying a third guard and two white inmates.

The "Zebra" trial in San Francisco offered no such mixed results. Brutal "Death Angels" Jessie Cooks, Larry Green, Manuel Moore and J. C. X. Simon stood convicted of first-degree murder and conspiracy involving multiple white victims slain at random. Alas, since California still hadn't restored capital punishment, the four received life sentences with possible parole.

Every cop's worst nightmare, the Black Liberation Army, still wouldn't lie down and play dead. One of its recent recruits, George Wright, had pled no contest to a holdup-murder back in 1963, receiving a sentence of fifteen to thirty years' imprisonment. In August 1970, with three other inmates, he'd escaped from New Jersey's Leesburg State Prison, fleeing in the warden's car. G-men started hunting Wright and fellow escapee George Brown for unlawful flight to avoid confinement, but they hadn't caught their men by July 31, 1972, when Wright, Brown, and five associates hijacked Delta Air Lines Flight 841 en route from Detroit to Miami.

Their plan was slick, Gantt had to give them that. Wright had boarded the plane disguised as a Catholic priest, packing a pistol inside a hollowed-out Bible. A third man, Melvin McNair, tagged along with wife Jean and two small children, while Brown's wife Joyce completed the team with their two-year-old son. Once airborne, the BLA gang seized control of the jet, redirecting it to Boston, then on to Algiers. Algerian authorities returned the plane and crew on August 2nd, but by then the hijackers had disappeared. Another hunt began, bagging Wright, the McNairs, Joyce Brown and her kid in Paris on May 26th of this year. Tried in France, Melvin

McNair and George Wright got three years apiece, while their wives received suspended sentences on account of the children. George Brown was still at large, presumably somewhere in Europe, with no further leads forthcoming to the FBI.

And then, Gantt thought, *there's always AIM.*

Nothing had changed for the better on South Dakota's Pine Ridge Reservation since the siege at Wounded Knee. Inhabitants of the rez. Dick Wilson was no longer tribal chairman, but critics kept charging purported members of his GOON squad with random brutality, rape and murder. The Bureau didn't bother with those charges, but it kept an eye on AIM for any little thing its members might be doing—such as possibly stealing an old pickup truck. Special Agents Jack Coler and Ronald Williams pursued one such junker, purportedly tracking wanted fugitives, and got themselves killed in a shootout on June 26, 1975, which put all hands-on deck and looking for payback.

Bureau lab reports, accurate or otherwise, seemed to finger four suspects. In February 1976 they'd traced alleged triggerman Leonard Peltier to Canada, where Mounties jailed him pending extradition. Peltier's lawyers were still fighting his transfer to the States, but meanwhile, prosecutors charged three other men with murdering Coler and Williams. Justice dug up a witness who claimed to be Peltier's girlfriend, but Peltier denied even knowing her. Defense attorneys for the other three defendants proved the state's witness was nowhere near the shooting scene, and in July jurors acquitted all three on grounds of self-defense.

To Gantt, it sounded like a kind of open season on G-men, making him glad that he no longer had to deal with bad guys in the field.

MICHAEL NEWTON

MONTEVIDEO, Uruguay: December 7, 1976

THE SHIFT to South America had come as a relief to Hardy
Gantt—at least, until he realized that continent was even
more screwed up than Southeast Asia. And he knew
damned well, although he'd never speak the truth aloud,
that meddling by the CIA had made matters immeasur-
ably worse.

In Argentina, for example, General Jorge Videla had
seized power back in March, imposing a military dictatorship that made the old Perón regime seem liberal. These
days, his nation not only waged "dirty war" against its
native dissidents, but also welcomed "death flights" from
the Pinochet junta in Chile, happily exterminating
malcontents Chileans didn't want to kill and plant at
home. Videla's Secretariat of Intelligence (SIDE) played
fast and loose with laws mandating human rights, when it
acknowledged them at all—another trait Videla's country
shared with Chile's Directorate of National Intelligence
(DINA). When not engaged in torturing and killing native
critics, both teams fielded hit squads that could strike as
far away as the United States and Europe with seeming
impunity.

Not that the deaths of communists caused Hardy any
sleepless nights, mind you. He rated that a cost of doing
business in the modern world, but did the men in charge
of Argentina and Brazil, Bolivia and Chile, Paraguay and
Uruguay give any thought at all to how their global killing
spree might cost them international allies?

Bernardo Leighton Guzmán was a case in point. A

former leader of Chile's Christian Democratic Party, Minister of State under three presidents before the Pinochet mob seized control, had been exiled to Europe with his family three years ago. DINA agents had tracked him to Rome last year, caught in the act of plotting his murder, but exposure didn't stop them. On October 6th of this year, "persons unknown" had shot Guzmán and his wife. Both survived, but Guzmán suffered permanent brain damage.

João Goulart had been Brazil's president when a military coup deposed him in 1964, choosing exile in Uruguay, of all places, over certain death in his homeland. Right-wing terrorists planned to snatch his son for ransom in March of this year, and while he'd moved to Argentina next, that only made things worse. Just yesterday, he had collapsed and died at his apartment in Mercedes, where authorities were calling it a heart attack. Agency sources leaned toward poison, but they'd never know for sure since Goulart was interred without an autopsy.

Nor was there any safety in numbers for doomed liberals. In May, Chilean exile Héctor Gutiérrez, onetime Speaker of the Chamber of Deputies, was found dead in a car, parked in Buenos Aires. With him were ex-senator Zelmar Michelini and two alleged Tupamaros militants, all tortured before they were shot. A month later, still in Buenos Aires, former Bolivian president Juan José Torres was kidnapped and murdered. CIA files suggested that DINA had killed all four, hiring mercenary Croatian terrorists for the wet work.

Nor did hit teams from South America avoid striking targets in the United States. CIA Director Bush had tipped New York congressman Ed Koch that DINA agents planned to kill him for proposing legislation that would cut off military aid to Uruguay. Despite the warning, neither Bush nor Clarence Kelley at the FBI would spare agents to cover Koch when he requested help. So far, at least, Koch had survived.

The same couldn't be said for exiled Chilean Minister of Defense Orlando Letelier. Imprisoned for a year after the Pinochet coup, upon release Letelier had taken his family to Venezuela, then to Washington, D.C., where he remained outspoken in defiance of Chile's dictatorship while serving as Director of Planning and Development for the liberal Institute for Policy Studies. On September 21st he was driving to work with IPS associate Ronni Moffitt and her husband Michael when their car exploded, leaving only Michael alive. FBI analysts identified bomb residue, and by now Langley knew the killer had been DINA hitmen Michael Townley and Fernandez Larios, dispatched for the job by General Manuel Contreras and Brigadier Pedro Espinoza Bravo. Paraguayan President Alfredo Stroessner—the same Nazi-lover presently sheltering fugitive war criminal Dr. Josef Mengele—had supplied the killers with phony passports and diplomatic visas a month before the Washington murders.

Still, as Hardy knew only too well, there was a world of difference between knowing something and proving it in court. From where he sat, the odds of extraditing, trying and convicting Letelier's killers—much less the men who'd ordered the bombing—were slim, as in zero.

Maybe, he thought, his time in South America would be both educational and just plain fun.

CHAPTER 4

New York City was *big*. Its five boroughs sprawled over 468 square miles and harbored 7.9 million full-time residents, whereas Chicago's 234 square miles claimed less than half as many citizens. Both dwarfed D.C., Erin O'Hara's birthplace, and in Gotham she felt like a truly tiny fish in shark-infested seas.

Another difference: while the Bureau's Chicago field office made do with one Special Agent in Charge, New York City had its own Assistant Director in Charge plus six—count 'em, *six*—SACs. Erin was so far down the totem pole she barely counted, yet she knew that scrutiny from her superiors might be relentless. Add to that the local cost of living, nearly twice the Windy City's, forcing Erin into a crappy one-room "studio" apartment in Brooklyn's Canarsie district, and she had to wonder if the transfer was a blessing or a curse thinly disguised.

The good news: on arrival her SAC—Jeb Bradshaw, forty-something but still fit—had moved O'Hara from her former posting with the Criminal Division to Counterintelligence, specifically what local agents called the "Russia desk." She'd met the other agents keeping watch for Soviet illegals, and while none of them were overjoyed to greet her, neither had they picked up where Chicago's crew left off, ragging on Erin for her father's testimony to the Church Committee that had bared the Bureau warts and all, with no airbrushing to disguise its faults.

So far, so good...or maybe they were just caught up in waiting for the other shoe to drop at headquarters.

Director Clarence Kelley had announced he was retiring at the end of February, prompting new President Jimmy Carter to find a replacement. Carter's first choice had been U.S. District Judge Frank Johnson from Alabama's Middle District, known for civil rights rulings that drove the Klan to bomb his mother's home in 1965, and while Johnson appeared to want the job, an aortic aneurysm forced him to decline. Carter was still looking, while Assistant Director James Blackburn Adams served as placeholder. A former Texas prosecutor and state legislator, Adams had quit politics in 1951 to join the Bureau and was SAC of San Antonio when Carter tapped him to fill Kelley's shoes pending selection of a permanent successor.

So far, no one could guess when that might happen, but for now Erin was happy to be hunting Russkies with a bunch of guys who didn't seem to hate her at first sight. The friendliest so far was Agent Stephen Barnes, whose affable demeanor in the office made O'Hara wonder how he'd manage in a confrontation on the street.

For now, Erin was hoping there'd be no need to find out.

———

"So, DID YOU SEE THE SPICKS?" Angelo Giordano asked, around a mouthful of calzone.

Dominic, his elder brother and boss of their family since Papa Carlo passed, watched Ange chomping his food and hoped that wasn't how he looked to other people when they saw him eating at some fancy restaurant.

"I saw 'em, yeah," he finally replied. "That same Bermúdez guy we met before, scars on his cheek like Al Capone."

"One ugly guy," Ange said.

"His product's got us sitting pretty though," Dom said. "I bumped our take to six keys monthly. Got a feeling that we're goin' places."

"Long as we don't wind up in a landfill," Ange replied.

"I've got it covered," Dom assured his sibling.

Still, the threat of sudden death was always something to consider in their line of work.

In March, one of Chicago's toughest shooters and a guy Dom had regarded as a friend, Charles Nicoletti, had been shot three times outside a restaurant in Northlake, Illinois. The suburb called itself "The City of Friendly People," but at least one of them didn't care much for Nicoletti. Even with three slugs in his head, the guy *mafiosi* called "Chuckie Typewriter," after his fondness for submachine guns, took seven hours to die, and Dom was curious about what random thoughts had crossed the mangled remnants of his mind while he was crossing over.

Now, since May, the Micks were acting up in Gotham, taking out each other and whichever wise guys they decided might be dangerous to keep around. On May 5th they'd lured Charles Stein—a loan shark owned by Fat Tony Salerno—to Jimmy Coonan's 596 Club on West 43rd Street and killed him there, reason unknown. Within a week of that hit, Coonan's shooters took out rival Westies leader Mickey Spillane—no relation to the writer, far as Dom knew—and secured Jimmy's hold on Hell's Kitchen.

Wars were never good for business in New York, but Dominic saw no threats from the Irish to his own domain, and if the coke kept flowing from Colombia, helping his family's war chest along, the Micks might even wind up being customers of his.

As long as he kept both eyes on their gun hands, right, and never lost sight of the fact that family, his own blood, was the foundation of trust.

And even that, in Dom's world, could be flexible.

————

CIA Headquarters: June 14, 1947

WHEN COLBY GANTT took time on rare occasions to review his life—age fifty-six, with thirty-five of those in service to the OSS and CIA—he recognized some hiccups on his chosen path but, overall, considered that it had been one hell of a ride.

More to the point, it wasn't over yet, even with changes in the wind.

In early March, retired Admiral Stansfield Turner, decorated hero of the Korean War and later president of the Naval War College, had replaced George Bush as CIA Director, while Bush went for the big bucks as chairman of the First National Bank in Houston. Four months after that, Congress created a new Permanent Select Committee on Intelligence chaired by Representative Edward Boland of Massachusetts. Although married for the first time five years earlier, at age sixty-one, Boland shared digs in Washington with fellow Bay State congressman Tip O'Neill, both of their wives staying at home.

Gantt didn't know what to make of that odd arrangement, but he was looking into it while waiting for liberal Boland to yank on the Agency's reins at the first opportunity.

One opening might be the recent revelations about MKULTRA, pouring forth from Boland's rivals with the Senate Select Committee on Intelligence. That panel had lately discovered 20,000 pages of classified Agency documents somehow missed when DCI Richard Helms purged Agency files back in 1973. The latest exposé included CIA plans to drug Castro prior to one of his public addresses, making him look like a nutcase. Other documents, summarized on the Senate floor by Senator Ted Kennedy —another Massachusite, or "Masshole" as Colby called him—listed more than thirty U.S. universities and hospitals engaged in MKULTRA's illegal drug testing "at all social levels, high and low," native Americans and foreign, including frequent dosing of "unwitting subjects in social situations."

MICHAEL NEWTON

When Gantt heard that, he had to wonder whether
Kennedy was thinking of his own scandal on Chap-
paquiddick Island eight years earlier, when he'd driven his
car off a bridge and then wandered off "in a daze" for ten
hours, leaving a young female "friend" to drown in the
submerged vehicle they'd been sharing well past
midnight.

MKULTRA was a mess, and most Americans still
didn't know the half of it, but Gantt was more concerned
about the House Select Committee on Assassinations
digging into JFK's demise in Dallas and the death of
Martin Luther King. Concerning Kennedy, Bulgarian
Dimitre Dimitrov had already briefed the Church
Committee on ties between Lee Harvey Oswald and
Russian émigré George de Mohrenschildt, further
claiming that he—Dimitrov—knew who'd ordered JFK's
death, but it appeared the HSCA was running short of
witnesses these days. On March 29th, shortly after
speaking to a committee investigator by phone, de
Mohrenschildt died from a shotgun blast to the head at
his Florida home. The local coroner called it a suicide.
Soon after that, Dimitrov—who'd once survived drugs
and torture while jailed by MKULTRA spooks in Panama
—vanished without a trace.

For his part, Colby wasn't betting on the blabber-
mouth returning short of Judgment Day.

Another walking, talking problem—for the moment,
anyway—was James Earl Ray, locked up for life and then
some in the King assassination. Ray's latest lawyer, Jack
Kershaw, had presented the HSCA with what he deemed
exculpatory evidence, then Ray had managed to escape
with seven other cons a short month later, from
Tennessee's remote Brushy Mountain State Penitentiary,

76

remaining at large for three days until they were recaptured yesterday.

While Ray received another year for the breakout, capping his sentence at an even century, HSCA's ballistics team had run tests on the shattered slug retrieved from Dr. King in 1968, reporting that it couldn't be matched to the rifle discarded on Main Street in Memphis moments after the assassination. Inconclusive data wouldn't get Ray out of prison, and now he was shopping around for another attorney, having fired Kershaw when he learned the lawyer had received $11,000 for arranging Ray's recent interview with *Playboy* magazine.

So, what the hell? As long as rank confusion ruled the day, Colby supposed he had no reason for concern about the spate of murders that had changed domestic politics forever between 1963 and '68. It was a good thing, too, considering the Hell on Earth that would consume whoever took the rap for killing off the American dream.

———

FBI Headquarters: July 5, 1977

Lately, Agent Devon Gantt had come to wonder if the FBI was actually making any strides against subversive groups in the United States, or if the Bureau's adversaries would turn out to be their own worst enemies.

Consider the Black Panthers. After his release from prison, Huey Newton had exiled himself to Cuba, where his message seemed to please Fidel Castro. Returning to the States this month, Huey had found some of the party's menfolk up in arms because they were outnumbered and outranked by female Panthers. Huey's solution: ordering some of the boys to beat Regina Davis, principal of the Panther school program in Oakland, for reprimanding a male subordinate, leaving her hospitalized with a broken jaw. Now women were quitting the party in droves, and it seemed Huey had screwed himself again.

Down in Los Angeles, Ron Karenga tried to revive his US Organizations by formulating a program called *Kawaida*—"normal" in Swahili—that called for his supporters to accept Karenga's view of secular humanism, dropping God from the concept of morality and self-fulfillment. He'd stopped beating female disciples—and, in fact, kept on denying that he ever had, a jury's guilty verdict notwithstanding—but some US adherents still clung to their parents' old-time religion and took offense at what they viewed as atheism.

MOVE was another story, still raising holy hell in Philadelphia despite a "treaty" with local police to minimize their status as a public nuisance. Agreements be damned, the cult kept stockpiling trash and blasting amplified rants around the clock from their communal digs on North 33rd Street in the city's Powelton Village district. Devon didn't like their chances of surviving in the neighborhood unless they managed to deescalate the situation, but the one thing that continued to elude leader "John Africa" was anything that smacked of common sense.

Reports from local cops kept claiming the Black Liberation Army was as good as dead, but members of the whacked-out group kept making trouble for themselves. Most recently, BLA gunman Russel Shoatz had escaped from Pennsylvania's Huntington Prison, where he'd been five years into a life term for murder. He'd scrounged a living from the streets and garbage dumpsters for a month, then carjacked a stranger and went on the lam till a state trooper caught him in a dramatic showdown, leaping on the stolen auto's hood to jam a gun in Shoatz's face. That meant more time for breaking out, but what was five or six years to a con already doing life?

The late George Jackson's Black Guerrilla Family presently seemed more or less defunct outside of prison walls, and on the inside it was taking hits from battling the hostile Aryan Nations. In April, Nazi cons had fatally stabbed BGF member Garland Berry, in retaliation for an attack on one of their own, and Gantt knew the spiral of violence was bound to get worse before it ended.

The year's big victory for Justice and the Bureau, if it could be called a win, was finally convicting Leonard Peltier for killing two G-men in 1975, on the Pine River Reservation. Some of the evidence was shaky, and the prosecution's witnesses had trouble sticking to a single version of events for more than two days in a row, but jurors bought the package, voting guilty on two counts of murder in the first degree, handing AIM's poster boy a couple of consecutive life sentences.

In all, not bad so far. As Gantt's late father Aloysius might've said, it didn't matter who brought down the bad guys, just as long as they went down and never had a chance to rise again.

————

MANHATTAN: July 8, 1977

A QUARTER PAST MIDNIGHT, and there was still ample traffic on West 39th Street as Agent Stephen Barnes approached the mail drop he had been assigned for contact with his KGB handler. The passing cars and wandering pedestrians didn't concern him, even though he had been watching for a tail throughout his subway ride to Times Square, disembarking there and walking seven blocks to the southwest on 7th Avenue to reach his designated drop, where he'd rented a post box in another name.

As far as Barnes could tell, no one from either side— the Bureau or the KGB—had followed him tonight, or on his other visits to the drop since he'd begun to feed Lieutenant Colonel Alexander Bobrik copies of selected files from the FBI office he served.

Tonight's lot, photographic negatives as usual, included surveillance reports on the Soviet consulate in Manhattan and Russia's embassy in Washington, along with documents detailing Bureau failure to detect a rumored nest of Stasi spies collaborating with the KGB in New York and New Jersey. Barnes had no idea if any of the documents he'd photographed so far were useful to the Soviets in any way, but envelopes of cash kept on arriving at his cover address, and for Stephen's purpose it was more the very act of leaking that he cherished.

Every document that found its way from Bureau files to Bobrik's hand was one more blow against the FBI, his father's hated nemesis and the now the sole target of Stephen's rage.

The only blip on his radar at work was a new agent transferred from Chicago and assigned to his own branch of the Counterintelligence Division. Barnes had sneaked a look at Erin O'Hara's personnel file and found nothing spectacular within its pages, no reason to think she'd been assigned specifically to search for outlaw leaks. The

Bureau transferred agents all the time—seemed to take pride, in fact, that it uprooted lives and families on short notice—so her appearance on the scene was not suspicious in itself.

Barnes recognized her as attractive, one year younger than himself and comely in her way, but he felt nothing for her in the way of sexual allure. Perhaps that was a failure of his personality, but he had never lusted after girls—or boys, for that matter—compelled throughout his college years to "play the field" like other male classmates, avoiding any notion that he might be "strange."

Today, aside from loose talk in the Bureau's locker room, who even cared?

When not searching the Bureau's files for information that might help the KGB, Barnes kept his eye on Mother Russia and her foreign satellites, with emphasis on dissidents who threatened harmony. On New Year's Day, for instance, 242 anticommunist Czechs had signed "Charter 77," essentially demanding broader human rights throughout their nation under President and Communist Party Secretary General Gustáv Husák. It bemused Barnes that the protest sprang from last December's arrest of a ludicrous psychedelic band called The Plastic People of the Universe. One band member had been deported, while others drew prison terms ranging from eight to eighteen months, and *that*, of all things, had provoked a challenge to communism nationwide.

In Moscow, meanwhile, Jewish chess master Natan Sharansky had been blasting Russian anti-Semitism since 1973, when he was denied a visa to play a championship match in Israel. Overnight he'd become an outspoken "refusenik"—one of 1,300 Jews who'd been denied passage to Israel since the latter 1940s, and had pressed his luck too far in March, arrested on multiple charges of treason and espionage. Facing a potential death sentence, Sharansky remained adamant, seizing any chance to broadcast propaganda from his cell, while Moscow's Ministry of Justice predicted trial early next year.

Why not just shoot him and be done with it? Barnes wondered, not that anyone back home had asked for his opinion.

Before entering his mail drop, Stephen took a long and searching look along the street, then ducked inside. Another night, one more betrayal of the Bureau he despised above all things, and yet another blow struck in his father's name.

———

DENVER, *Colorado: November 16, 1977*

SPECIAL AGENT WYMAN GANTT was hunting for a fugitive and couldn't find him anywhere. David Gilbert, age thirty-three, had been one of Columbia University's original SDS members, later switching to the violent Weatherman Underground, with a hodgepodge of charges filed against him since he'd dropped from sight two years ago. Now rumors placed him back in Denver, where he'd organized a WU collective in October 1969, but while putative sightings continued, Gantt still hadn't spotted Gilbert in the flesh.

He would have given up by now, but orders from on high controlled his movements these days, since the undercover "Beards" unit had been disbanded by headquarters, even though it seemed his mission hadn't changed.

Another fugitive on Wyman's list was Marilyn Jean Buck, a Texas native known for feminist poetry and her editorship of *The Rag,* an underground newspaper once published by the SDS chapter at Austin's university. After switching to the Weathermen, she'd logged a ten-year prison term in 1973 for using fake I.D. to purchase otherwise legal ammunition. Four years later, some fool had granted her a work furlough and she'd never returned. Gantt suspected her involvement with the group's Prairie Fire Organizing Committee's magazine *Breakthrough*, but he couldn't prove it, much less tell his fellow G-men where to find Buck and return her to prison.

Nationwide, most talking heads on TV thought the WU was dead and gone. The leftist John Brown Book Club, distributors of *Breakthrough,* had published a kind of farewell pamphlet this spring, titled *The Split of the Weather Underground Organization: Struggling against White and Male Supremacy.* "White" and "male" were virtually dirty words these days, with what remained of the New Left, but Wyman didn't share the general consensus that the Weathermen were down and out.

So far this very month, in fact, WU member Matthew Steen had appeared on the lead segment of CBS TV's *Sixty Minutes,* telling the program's audience that fugitive Weathermen would soon "re-emerge and engage change at the community level." When Mark Rudd surfaced, it was only to surrender on charges related to the 1970 Greenwich Village townhouse explosion, but others were clearly planning new actions. Just days ago, police had busted five Prairie Fire Organizing Committee members for plotting to bomb the Orange County office of Republican California State Senator John Briggs. Four of the five were talking plea bargains, while only one looked forward to a jury trial.

However that turned out, Gantt knew that there would be no peace in the United States as long as any leftist radicals remained at large, unsupervised. He missed the heady COINTELPRO days when ends had justified the Bureau's means...and who could say, if bloody strife continued, that those good old days might not return?

————

ROCK CREEK PARK, Washington, D.C.: November 15, 1977

NOLAN O'HARA HOPED a nice long walk would clear his head of visions rife with death. He'd seen his share of it while serving with the FBI, from Ku Klux terrorism to a Mississippi cop shot down during a raid that should've been avoided, but the death roiling his mind this week wasn't a killing he had personally witnessed. Still, he'd known the victim—or known *of* him—and was questioning reports that called it accidental.

Wild Bill Sullivan was dead, shot down near his retirement home at Sugar Hill, New Hampshire, five years after his curt dismissal from the FBI for locking horns with Edgar Hoover, only days before his scheduled House Select Committee on Assassinations testimony.

Grafton County officers were calling it an accident. They claimed that Sullivan was on his way to rendezvous with hunting pals when a high-powered rifle slug ripped through his neck, killing him almost instantly. The confessed shooter, a state policeman's twenty-something son, reported that it wasn't daylight when he'd spotted movement in the forest through his rifle's telescopic sight and shot what he believed to be a deer. There was no word yet as to whether Sullivan was wearing "hunter orange" when he went down—protective garb recommended though not required by New Hampshire's Fish and Game Department—but the triggerman would face a hefty find for negligence and probably suspension of his hunting license when another season rolled around.

But none of that helped Sullivan, and if his death somehow *wasn't* an accident, its impact could be stifling on other witnesses subpoenaed by Congress to spill whatever they might know about the JFK and King assassinations.

One thing Nolan knew, from digging on his own: Sullivan's death wouldn't prevent the publication of a memoir he'd recently completed, scheduled for release from W. W. Norton sometime during the next year or so.

What secrets would the book reveal?

He was distracted when a male voice called out from behind him? "Nolan? Nolan O'Hara?"

Pausing in mid-stride, O'Hara turned to face the speaker and beheld a husky fellow somewhere in his thirties, sandy hair cropped short, round-faced, his eyes concealed behind a pair of mirrored sunglasses like those the prison walking boss had worn in *Cool Hand Luke* some years ago. He wore a two-piece jogging suit bearing the Nike logo on the zippered jacket, both hands thrust into that garment's pockets. He was smiling slightly, like an old acquaintance wondering if Nolan would remember him.

Thinking about the .38 he wore beneath his own coat, difficult to reach with it buttoned, O'Hara asked, "And you are...?"

"Not important," said the stranger. "Just a messenger."

"So, what's the message?"

Now the man withdrew his right hand, leveling a small black automatic pistol. "Nothing much," the man replied. "Just this: you should've stopped while there was time."

O'Hara didn't have to ask precisely what he should have stopped. Instead, he tried to reach his gun but didn't make it. Two flat *cracks* echoed among the trees surrounding him, then he was falling face down on the hiking path, surprised to feel so little pain.

BIRMINGHAM, *Alabama: November 19, 1977*

DAVE JORDAN HADN'T HEARD from Fee O'Hara since she'd flown to Washington for yet another funeral—her brother, this time, clearly murder rather than an accident as with her father on the last occasion. Dave had driven her to Birmingham International Airport for a red-eye flight across country, with no idea of when—or even if—she would return.

He knew too well the impact murder had on families, made worse when law enforcement had no clues to work with and no realistic hope of getting justice. With the Giordano Family that spawned him, losing one of David's uncles and his father to successive gangland wars, at least there was sometimes the fleeting satisfaction of revenge outside the law. But in a case like this...

Jordan had begged off with a plea of pending cases, and Fiona hadn't seemed to mind flying alone. Whether she was concealing pent-up anger at him, Dave couldn't have said, but meeting the O'Haras who remained over another grave had struck him as too much, particularly after Nolan—the deceased this time—had spilled the truth about Dave's family and brought their up-and-down relationship to its worst crisis point.

And there was ample news of ghastly deaths to go around in Birmingham.

Bill Baxley, coming off his failure to imprison Klansmen who had murdered Willie Edwards long ago, was up at bat once more, this time against a Klansman he'd indicted for the bombing that had killed four young black girls in 1963. Almost predictably, defendant Robert Chambliss had retained the closest thing in Alabama these days to a Klan attorney: Art Hanes Sr., onetime racist mayor of Birmingham, defender in their turn of Kluxers who'd murdered civil rights worker Viola Liuzzo in '65, alleged assassin James Earl Ray three years later, and between the two, a group of Klansmen charged with sundry felonies in North Carolina.

Hanes fought for his clients as the Constitution required, denying all the while that he was racist, never mind the times as mayor when he'd denounced "niggers" at White Citizens' Council rallies. Sometimes he won acquittals, but this wasn't one of them.

For starters, FBI headquarters had grudgingly released its 1960s "BAPBOM" file, including a memo identifying the church bombers as Chambliss, Herman Cash, Bobby Cherry, and Tom Blanton Jr. Despite informers' statements and a heap of other evidence, they'd closed the case without prosecution on 1968, by order of Director Edgar Hoover.

Why? Had it been Hoover's lifelong racism, his firm if

deluded belief that any blacks demanding equal rights were "communists"? Or had the old man simply been afraid of losing if the case had gone to trial, his precious FBI embarrassed in the blazing light of international publicity?

What did it even matter now?

Baxley had managed to convict Chambliss on one of four murder counts—for killing eleven-year-old Carol McNair—with the guilty verdict handed down two days after what would've been his victim's twenty-sixth birthday. The resultant sentence of life imprisonment likely didn't mean much to Chambliss, a chain-smoking drunkard at seventy-three, but there'd been celebrations in the local black community, coupled with calls for prosecution of the other terrorists who still survived.

That said, Chambliss was free on $20,000 bond pending appeal by Hanes and son, but that might take another year or more to navigate the standard legal maze. If Chambliss lived that long, it would be comforting to see him die in prison, but Dave had to wonder how many others just like him still walked free, convinced they'd never face a jury.

Never mind, he thought. *It's too damned late to switch and turn into a prosecutor now.*

And if he tried, would any living members of his family still speak to him?

———

HARLEM: November 23, 1977

Tomorrow was Thanksgiving, and it irritated Sergeant Payton Sawyer that he dreaded spending time with the small remnant of his family. His sister and his niece were fine in small doses, maybe phone calls one a month or so, but sitting down with them for dinner tested Sawyer's patience to the limit with their jabber that boiled down to "Me-Me-Me." They never seemed to care about what might be happening in Payton's life—the parts that he was free to talk about, at least.

For instance, he'd been following the civil rights lawsuit filed in Chicago by Fred Hampton's family, alleging wrongful death from 1969 when he was first drugged by an FBI *agent provocateur,* then murdered in his sleep by racist cops. Payton had lost his younger brother in the same so-called "shootout"—and Fred was Keisha's brother too, her daughter's uncle—but did either of them ask about the case? Hell, no. Payton had turned thumbs down on joining in the suit, despite repeated overtures, and now Judge Joseph Perry had dismissed the claim after a jury deadlocked.

Justice? Sawyer shook his head and finished off his second beer.

Meanwhile, he kept track of the many charges filed against Black Liberation Army "den mother" JoAnne Chesimard. In April, something called the Easter Coalition for Human Rights had purchased an ad in the *New York Times,* listing Chesimard—or "Assata Shakur," as she now called herself—among several self-proclaimed political prisoners. Around the same time, a panel of international jurists touring U.S. prisons reported to the United Nations Commission on Human Rights that Chesimard's solitary cell in a prison for male convicts was "totally unbefitting any prisoner." America's federal courts didn't care, Judge Clarkson Fisher rejecting Chesimard's request for a transfer to Clinton Correctional Facility for

Women, his judgment approved by the Third Circuit Court of Appeals.

Even so, Chesimard and her lawyers kept chipping away at the government's long list of charges against her. She'd been convicted in March for the New Jersey Turnpike shootout, found guilty on eight counts, with first-degree murder the only one that really mattered. On the flip side, October saw her 1972 charges of murder and robbery from a Bronx social club dropped, and only yesterday another dismissal had cleared her of attempted robbery at the Statler Hilton Hotel in 1971.

Games lawyers play. Payton shrugged off the losses, content with Chesimard's life sentence in New Jersey, and got up to fetch himself another beer.

———

Buenos Aires, Argentina: December 16, 1977

Buenos Aires translates as "good air" or "fair winds," and Hardy Gantt couldn't argue with that. Situated on Argentina's Atlantic coast, the nation's capital benefited from polar air dubbed *sudestada*—"southeast blows"—that commonly ensured moderate temperatures year round. That said, heat had been known to spike above 100 degrees in summer, which made Gantt thankful for steady access to cold alcoholic beverages.

This afternoon he was dawdling at a sidewalk café in the city's upscale Palermo Chico district, waiting for a dodgy informer who might or might not have information on surviving remnants of the far-left Peronist Armed Forces, a revolutionary band having as much in common with its neo-Nazi namesake as chalk did with cheese. The guy was running late, and Gantt ordered another margarita while he waited, hoping that he wouldn't be stood up.

His job in South America these days was keeping Langley briefed on Operation Condor's bloody progress, helping the regime strike more effectively against potential enemies. Fluke storms this year had littered Buenos Aires beaches with hundreds of corpses dumped at sea, horrifying tourists and reviving heated protests against babies kidnapped by the military for adoption by rich childless couples nationwide and abroad. Vanished children had noisy advocates dubbed Mothers of the Plaza de Mayo, clamoring for answers while President Jorge Rafael Videla branded the movement subversive. To prove that point, his soldiers had kidnapped the group's founder, with two French nuns, torturing and killing all three before burying them at sea.

No matter where Gantt looked in Latin America, it seemed to be the same old story. Six thousand miles to the north, in El Salvador, General Carlos Humberto Romero had captured the presidency for his National Conciliation Party, in an election marked by wholesale fraud and intimidation of voters by army-sponsored goon squads brandishing machetes. When protests erupted in San Salvador, Romero's troops turned out and opened fire, claiming they'd "only" killed 200 dissidents. Conflicting press reports bumped the number to 1,500 and spawned armed resistance from a new Farabundo Martí National Liberation Front.

Clearly, with Nicaragua's Sandinista National Liberation Front going strong and other leftist movements on the rise, there'd be no shortage of Latin American wars for the foreseeable future. All Gantt had to do was assess and dive in, as Langley might require.

Checking his watch, with half his second margarita gone, Hardy decided he would give his spook another fifteen minutes, then move on to something else. And if the no-show still wanted handouts from Uncle Sam, he could kneel down and beg like everybody else.

CHAPTER 5

SERGEANT PAYTON SAWYER, pushing fifty, had about decided that he'd risen to the highest NYPD rank he'd ever attain. He'd taken the lieutenant's test, passing each one but ranking so far down the list that half of his superiors would have to quit the force or die before he was promoted. He'd heard women lately, talking on the TV news about "glass ceilings," but he wasn't sure what his dilemma might be called.

Maybe the curse of being stuck so long in BOSS?

Whatever.

Sawyer hoped, at least, that he was seeing the Black Liberation Army in its death throes. Hate like that would never die on either side, Payton supposed, but if the BLA was finally eliminated, maybe cops could go out on patrol without the fear of a deliberate assassination added to the other risks they faced each day and night.

The last BLA member making news so far this year,

predictably, was JoAnne Chesimard. Two weeks ago, she'd won her long court fight after a fashion, being transferred from her solitary cell at all-male Garden State Correctional Facility in Yardsdale to the a women's maximum-security unit at Alderson Federal Prison Camp in West Virginia, where she'd shared uneasy space with the Aryan Sisterhood and two Manson "family" alumni, Sandra Good and Lynette "Squeaky" Fromme.

That hadn't lasted long—the unit closed for good a week after Chesimard landed—and now she was locked up at Jersey's Clinton Correctional Facility for Women, presumably for the rest of her life, or until some future governor who didn't care about extending his political career broke down and granted clemency.

Like that would ever happen, right. The prospect was so ludicrous that Sawyer nearly laughed aloud.

With any luck, before Chesimard or any of her male BLA cohorts hit the street against, he'd be retired and living somewhere warm, like Florida or Southern California. But was there truly anyplace to hide from racial strife in the United States?

If so, he hadn't found it yet and doubted that he ever would.

———

FBI FIELD OFFICE, Manhattan: April 11, 1978

IT WAS a new day at the FBI, at least for some, but Agent Erin O'Hara still wasn't convinced that real change could take root and flourish.

The immediate good news: after a year of searching,

President Carter had finally found a new Bureau director, confirmed by the Senate on February 23rd. William Hedgecock Webster, fifty-four years old, had been a naval lieutenant in World War Two, then practiced law before appointment as U.S. Attorney for Missouri's Eastern District in 1960, followed by a five-year stint with the state's Board of Legal Examiners. President Nixon had appointed him to the federal bench in 1970, then to the Eighth Circuit Court of Appeals three years later. Jimmy Carter thought enough of him to pick Webster despite the fact that he was a Republican.

As director, Webster seemed to favor building cases that would never have been opened during Edgar Hoover's time. Instead of just collecting dirt that he could use to blackmail crooked politicians, Webster ordered agents to investigate them with an eye toward prosecution. Only days after his confirmation he'd approved an operation codenamed "ABSCAM" in New York, hiring paroled swindler and con man Melvin Weinberg with his girlfriend of the moment to create a front called "Abdul Enterprises" (which explained ABSCAM tag), Weinberg posing as the middleman for fictional Arab sheikhs—G-men in costume—who couldn't wait to bribe any and all available U.S. politicians. So far, the phony Arabs were discussing deals to "own" Atlantic City's three largest casinos, and where the trail would lead from there, nobody knew.

At the same time, Webster and Attorney General Griffin Bell were cleaning house and owning up to past Bureau mistakes. Yesterday, a federal grand jury had indicted ex-Director Patrick Gray, former Associate Director Mark Felt, and Deputy Assistant Director of the Inspections Division Edward Miller for crimes they'd

ordered and covered up during the scandalous COIN-
TELPO era. In the indictment's words, they "Did unlaw-
fully, willfully, and knowingly combine, conspire,
confederate, and agree together and with each other to
injure and oppress citizens of the United States who were
relatives and acquaintances of the Weatherman fugitives,
in the free exercise and enjoyments of certain rights and
privileges secured to them by the Constitution and the
laws of the United States of America."

So far, Gray was stalling for time, Felt claimed to be
"shocked," and Edwards fell back on the specious claim of
"just following orders." At their arraignment, 700 past and
present agents had turned out to applaud the so-called
"Washington Three."

Another positive change, in Erin's mind, was closure
of the Bureau's scandal-ridden Top Echelon Informant
Program, under which non-Italian mobsters had been
given a free pass—up to and including frame-ups of innocent victims for murders the favored felons committed—
in a quest for dirt that would convict Mafia members.
Since 1962 it seemed, the FBI had done a 180-degree turnaround from denying organized crime's existence to
coddling and climbing in bed with certain gangsters,
mostly Irishmen like Boston's Winter Hill Gang led by
serial murderer James "Whitey" Bulger.

In place of selected "Top Echelon" rats, Director
Webster had launched a broadly-based Criminal Informant Program that collected information from squealers
nationwide, with an eye toward convicting worse heavies
regardless of race, creed, or color.

There'd also been advancements on the scientific
front, from creation of a Behavioral Science Unit at Quan-
tico, analyzing and tracking psychopathic murderers, to

the FBI Laboratory's adoption of laser technology to detect fingerprints at crime scenes. Overall, Director Webster's stress on "quality" investigations, versus Hoover's lifelong obsession with often deceptive statistics, seemed to be working.

Still, as a G-woman, O'Hara wondered if equality would ever truly filter down to female agents and other minorities on the Bureau payroll before the twin issues of racism and sexism began snapping at Washington's heels.

———

Evanston, Illinois: May 27, 1978

SPECIAL AGENT WYMAN GANTT was no longer a Bureau "Beard," but he was still on the same mission, more or less. It didn't matter that the Weather Underground had basically disbanded, Jimmy Carter offering blanket amnesty to Vietnam-era draft evaders, signing off on a deal that gave ex-fugitive Mark Rudd a walk with two years' probation and a $4,000 fine.

But still, someone was out there making bombs.

Gantt didn't know if it would prove to be a trend or not, and so far no one had claimed credit for the latest bombing, but the blast had brought him here, to the main campus of Northwestern University, where income from sponsored research—military, corporate, whatever—topped $600 million yearly. Northwestern claimed America's ninth-largest university endowment, pushing $10 billion, and somebody obviously hated that idea.

The parcel bomb in question was tricky. Found in a parking lot at Chicago's University of Illinois, it bore the return address of engineering professor Buckely Crist at Northwestern, returned to his office by a helpful university staffer on May 25th. Crist knew immediately that he hadn't sent the package, so he gave it to campus security, and Officer Terry Marker opened it, setting off a charge that injured his left hand, with other minor cuts and burns.

What mattered, to Gantt's way of thinking, was the bomb itself. As reconstructed, it turned out to be a metal pipe nine inches long and one inch in diameter, each end sealed with handmade wooden plugs, versus the screw-on caps employed on most pipe bombs. The primitive trigger consisted of a nail and rubber bands, rigged to strike six common match heads and ignite the powder charge when the parcel was opened. Dumb luck, more than skilled planning, had prevented a misfire.

Other agents and local police were digging into Professor Crist's life and background, searching for someone who might hold a grudge worth killing for, but Gantt suspected they would come up empty. He had a hunch—nothing more, but just maybe enough—that the bomber would choose other targets in future, and perhaps would tip his hand by getting chatty with the press.

Was he or she political? Maybe. Northwestern had more than its fair share of government contracts, some with military applications, and the perp might even be someone outraged by private research, such as medical or cosmetic testing on caged animals. Gantt couldn't say yet, but he hoped to be around for next time, and perhaps the next one after that.

If it had legs, that was the kind of case that could be great for his career.

_____

LITTLE ITALY, Manhattan: June 8, 1978

ANGELO GIORDANO DID a double-take and asked his brother, "Why 'n hell you watchin' niggers on TV?"

Dominic glowered at him, pointed toward the Sony's screen, and said, "This guy ain't just a nigger. He's a congressman."

"No shit?" Angelo seemed truly surprised. "I thought the only one was that spade preacher outa Harlem, kicked the bucket five, six years ago. That Adam Who's-it."

"Clayton Powell," Dom finished for him. "Now clam up, will ya, and lemme listen?"

"What's your problem?" Ange asked him, sounding offended as he headed for the kitchen to retrieve a beer.

"It ain't my problem yet," Dom said. "But if these guys keep diggin', who knows where the shit might wind up landing."

"Which shit would that be, exactly?"

"Jesus, don't you ever pay attention? Shit from the assassinations, man."

"That don't narrow it down much, bro'."

"For Christ's sake, JFK and King."

"Which King?" Ange asked, and Dom wondered if he was only playing dumb now.

"King, the civil rights guy."

"Figures, with a nigger lookin' into it."

"They're lookin' at *La Cosa Nostra*, dummy. Get your head outa your ass."

"Like how?"

"Today they're grillin' *Don* Santo from Tampa, askin'

him about the CIA, Cuba, and some shit people claim he said about Kennedy back in Sixty-three, predicting he was gonna take a bullet."

"Santo's tellin' fortunes now? I always thought he looked a little like a Gypsy."

"He's denyin' it, but who knows what'll come of it, considerin' the other shit in Florida?"

Just days ago, a federal grand jury in Miami had indicted twenty-odd defendants including labor union guys and personnel from shipping companies, claiming they'd been involved in kickback schemes for moving cargo up and down along the whole East Coast. The G-men called it "Operation UNIRAC," for *union racketeer-*ing, and what else was new? Dom figured every waterfront in the U.S. was riddled with corruption, as they'd always been.

But now, the double-whammy: *mafiosi* nervous about going down were cleaning house, eliminating any possible informers. The latest, right here in New York, was Tony Provenzano's right-hand man and maybe shooter on the Jimmy Hoffa deal, knocked off to silence him. Dom knew him fairly well, as Sally Bugs, although his parents had named him Salvatore Briguglio.

And who'd be next? Maybe a certain fellow Dom saw peering from his bathroom mirror when he shaved, neck-deep in smuggling cocaine from Colombia.

"Just watch your step is all I'm sayin'," he told Angelo. "And watch your fuckin' back."

———

FBI Headquarters: August 10, 1978

.　.　.

SUBVERSIVES EVERYWHERE KEPT Agent Devon Gantt employed. The Bureau might be favored with new director, but he hadn't called off Gantt's surveillance of the Left, although it wasn't cool to speak of COINTELPRO anymore, when three of his onetime superiors might well be on their way to jail for fighting terrorists.

Race was the fuse that still sputtered and hissed across America, looking for buried charges waiting to explode. July had brought a race riot to Duel Vocational Institute in Tracey, California, and Black Guerrilla Family member Khatari Gaulden died at San Quentin on August 1st, after prison authorities refused him medical treatment for a head injury suffered while playing football.

One week later, in Philadelphia the MOVE cult had faced police in an hour-long standoff, one cop killed accidentally by brother officers, eighteen other persons wounded, and nine cult members—all named "Africa," of course—sentenced to life imprisonment on a dubious conviction of third-degree murder. The group survived without its so-called martyrs and continued going strong, blasting its nonsense over bullhorns to infuriate neighbors in Powellton Village.

And then, of course, there were the activists of AIM, still claiming Leonard Peltier was framed for double murder on the Pine Ridge Reservation. His appeals were going nowhere, but the group had launched what it referred to as the "Longest Walk"—a name hijacked from Mao Zedong no less—traipsing from a "sacred" peace pipe ritual on Alcatraz, across the continent to D.C., where they'd pitched tipis around the Washington Monument, protesting ancient treaty violations and a dozen laws they claimed discriminated against Indians. Devon could see their campfires from the rooftop of the Hoover Building if he bothered going up there, which was seldom.

All he had to know was that his father had been right: the more things changed, the more they stayed the same.

———

Birmingham, Alabama: September 22, 1978

"I can't believe he wrote *another* one," Fiona said. "Jesus, I can't believe they actually *published* it."

The book in question, as Dave Jordan knew too well, was yet another novel from faux Native American "Forrest" Carter, this one a fictionalized biography of Apache war chief Geronmo titled *Watch for Me on the Mountain.* Despite exposing Carter as a former Klansman with a violent past, no more "Indian" than Jordan was, critics were still enthusing over this, his latest pack of lies.

"Have you seen *Kirkus*?" asked Fiona.

"Not yet," Dave replied, noting she had the semi-monthly magazine already opened to the page she clearly planned on reading.

"Listen to this shit, will you? They call it 'history played for tragedy—less than totally enthralling or convincing but vivid, richly colored, and often fiercely effective.' I mean, *honestly!*"

"You know they charge authors and publishers for those reviews, right?" Dave reminded her. "They won't 'promise' positive results, but who pays cash up front to see their latest product slammed?"

"I know, okay? But most people have never heard that. They read *this*"—she gave the rumpled magazine a shake

—"and go out shopping for the next best-seller, while this bastard with the fake name rolls in money."

"Drinking most of it, from what I hear."

"I hope he chokes on it."

"Wouldn't surprise me." Jordan tried to change the subject. "Is there any new word on your brother's case?"

Meaning her brother's murder ten months earlier, in Washington. She'd come back from the funeral, surprising Dave a bit at that, but mostly shied away from any talk about the crime.

"Nothing," she said, tersely. "The cops still think it was a random mugging. Who shoots someone for their watch and wallet, Dave?"

"Sadly, for what I hear, a lot of people. More back east than here, even."

"I don't believe it," said Fiona, shaking her head. "Not when he was involved so closely with the House investigation into JFK and Dr. King."

Jordan had heard it all before and knew he couldn't help. Fiona had to fight this demon on her own, and Dave could only hope it wouldn't get the best of her.

———

CIA HEADQUARTERS: September 29, 1978

EVERY TIME he read a newspaper these days, or turned a television on, Colby Gantt wondered if it was time for him to quit the Agency. His twin brother was hanging in there with the FBI, but Colby had begun to think the whole charade was just a futile waste of time.

Nothing around him ever seemed to change, or if it did, that change was for the worse.

Take Albino Luciani for example, installed as Pope John Paul I on August 26th, dead thirty-three days later at age sixty-five. He'd come to office with a list of goals including revisions of canon law, promoting "dialogue," and encouraging world peace and social justice. Now look at where that landed him.

Conflicting statements from the Vatican couldn't decide who'd found his corpse in bed, what he'd been reading when he died, or whether there would be an autopsy to pinpoint cause of death. His list of enemies within the church was long, mostly conservatives within the College of Cardinals who saw their traditional beliefs, their tenure, and their lives of luxury imperiled by the new pontiff in town. Rumors of poisoning had already begun to circulate, some whispering about links between right-wing terrorism, the Mafia, and heavy Vatican investments in the scandal-ridden Banco Ambrosiano. Bank president Roberto Calvi was under investigation, as were certain members of *Propaganda Due*—"P2"—a branch of Freemasonry tied to Calvi's bank and terroristic acts, some of its adherents ruling Vatican City as members of the Roman Curia, despite their church's ban on joining the lodge. Luciani's replacement: Polish Cardinal Karol Józef Wojtyła, installed as Pope John Paul II.

The whole truth about that mess might never be revealed, and at the moment Colby worried more about the House Select Committee on Assassinations looking into matters that were better left alone. Some of the panel's recent witnesses included mobsters Santo Trafficante Jr., Lewis McWillie, Lennie Patrick, and Sam Campisi all hedging their bets, some admitting casual acquaintance with Jack Ruby, pleading the Fifth about anything else.

One odd note that disturbed Gantt was ex-New Orleans D.A. Jim Garrison's election as a judge to Louisiana's 4th Circuit Court of Appeal. The Clay Shaw trial and bad press linking Garrison to the Marcello family, including trial on bribery charges in 1973, wasn't enough to keep Big Easy voters from choosing Garrison over his Republican rival. He'd bear further watching, obviously, but with any luck at all, the HSCA might be led astray and feed Americans more pap to help them sleep at night.

Meanwhile, the truth was giving Gantt bad dreams.

———

FBI FIELD OFFICE, Manhattan: December 25, 1978

A FEMALE VOICE asked Agent Stephen Barnes, "You volunteer or draw the short straw?"

Turning in his swivel chair, Barnes saw Agent Erin O'Hara standing six feet from him, offering a tentative smile. He faked one in return and said, "My choice. I would've gone home to New Jersey, but my parents took a Christmas cruise to Puerto Rico."

Sneaking photographs of U.S. military bases on the tropic island for their Russian handler, though Barnes kept that bit to himself. Mark and Isabella Barnes were sleeper agents who had raised him as their own and still kept working for the KGB though in their sixties, with Mark's blood pressure a matter of concern.

"That must be nice," O'Hara said. "To get away."

"I guess. Truth is, I've never been much of a traveler," Barnes said.

Unless you counted coming all the way from Moscow to New Jersey as a child, and that was strictly off the record.

Suddenly, O'Hara shifted gears, saying, "So now, Afghanistan."

"Looks like it," Barbes replied.

In April, assassins had slain Mir Akbar Khyber, founding leader of the People's Democratic Party of Afghanistan, and communist Minister of Foreign Affairs Hafizullah Amin emerged from chaos as the nation's new president, backed by the Kremlin as he threatened harsh suppression of opponents. As Barnes learned from his KGB controller, that had opened the door for CIA support of rebellious, semi-autonomous tribal groups—and, not so incidentally, vastly expanding Afghan opium production. President Amin ordered a crackdown, while the CIA armed and financed Sunni mujahideen guerrillas, taking its cut of the heroin trade in exchange. That was too much for Moscow to take lying down, and Soviet diplomats advanced a treaty on December 5th, allowing deployment of troops in Afghanistan "at the government's request." Just this morning, one day short of three weeks later, President Amin had duly requested invasion, comfortable in his palace while Red Army troops flooded the countryside.

"I'll bet the CIA is loving this," O'Hara said.

"No doubt. More work for us, as well."

"Speaking of which, I'd better get back to it," Erin said, and offered him another smile before she moved off toward her office cubicle.

I'll have to keep an eye on that one, Stephen thought. *And make damned sure she doesn't find out what's been going on right here, under her nose.*

———

CIA AGENT HARDY GANTT had moved on to a new hemisphere, but echoes of his time in Southeast Asia kept drawing him back to his first foreign tour of duty. Yesterday morning, war had broken out between Democratic Kampuchea—formerly Cambodia—and Vietnam, as Vietnam's troops crossed the border in force, seeking to topple the Khmer Rouge regime based in Phnom Penh. Settling that mess could take a while, and Gantt was happy to be out of it.

And as it was, he had his plate full in El Salvador, the smallest and most densely populated country in Central America. Troops fielded by General Carlos Humberto Romero Mena, the nation's current president, had killed 687 civilians this year, according to Christian Legal Assistance, a Catholic legal aid society and El Salvador's leading human rights group, with no end to slaughter in sight.

At that, Hardy thought, Salvadorans should count themselves lucky not to live in Latin America's other hot spots. Operation Condor was still wreaking havoc from Brazil to Uruguay, where intergovernmental collaboration allowed Brazilian troops to kidnap an activist family of four from Porto Allegre in November. Chile had finally released DINA assassin Michael Townley into U.S. custody, but he wouldn't be punished for killing Orlando

Letelier or anyone else, once he'd vanished into the Federal Witness Protection Program as an informer against his ex-masters.

Langley had full knowledge of the slaughter going on throughout the "Southern Cone" of the Americas—had bankrolled and approved a major portion of it, if the truth be told—which, Hardy realized, would never happen.

How could anyone in Washington freely admit to all that shit?

Secrets? No problem, Hardy thought. *They've always been my family's stock in trade.*

CHAPTER 6

COLBY GANTT PAGED through his copy of the *Final Assassination Report* from Congress and figured it could have been worse. The panel's majority claimed both JFK and Dr. King were "probably" assassinated by conspirators five years apart, but after three years on the job, they'd barely scratched the surface.

With Kennedy, they'd dug up ancient sound recordings made in Dealey Plaza sixteen years ago, reporting that more shots were audible than those acknowledged by the Warren Commission. They'd dipped a toe into the murky pond of Jack Ruby's lifelong underworld connections, admitted Lee Oswald knew David Ferrie from his youth, that Ferrie was "apparently" a rabid anti-Castroite, and that Oswald was seen with Ferry, "if not Clay Shaw," as late as September 1963. The volume rehashed stories of CIA assassinations abroad, scolded the FBI for hiding its ties to Oswald in '63, and lightly slapped the Secret Service's wrist for procedural failings. Still...

Concerning Shaw, ex-Agency Director Richard Helms had granted under oath that dear, departed Clay had been a longtime operative of the CIA's Domestic Contact Service, like some 150,000 other Americans, but few of those received the "five Agency" security clearance bestowed on Shaw in 1949, three years after the army had discharged him as a major.

That aside, the groups deemed "not involved" in killing Kennedy included the Agency, FBI and Secret Service, Russia's government and Cuba's, and anti-Castro fighters "as a group." Nor was the Mob, they said, although "available evidence does not preclude the possibility that individual members may have been involved."

At least professional nay-sayer Amos Guidry hadn't modified his "no conspiracy" mantra since the report's publication. As he'd told a recent interviewer, "I'm not saying there wasn't a conspiracy. I know most people in this country believe there was a conspiracy. I just refuse to accept it and that's my life's work." A frank admission of his bias, even if the double-talk made Colby smile.

The committee got more specific about Dr. King. While insisting that James Earl Ray was the killer, it suggested without any solid evidence that his two brothers had supported him while he was traveling around the country and abroad between April 1967 and June 1968. Ray's motive, they declared, was "probably" a bounty placed on King by two rich Missouri bigots, both now conveniently dead. Ray "likely" heard about the open contract while he was in prison, then broke out and spent a year traipsing around North America before shooting King in the vague hope of collecting maybe-money from two men he'd never met, who'd never heard of him.

And if you buy that, Colby thought, *give my regards to Santa Claus.*

One guy who wouldn't be spilling the beans about Memphis was John Paul Spica, an associate of St. Louis godfather Anthony Giordano named in some conspiracy theories as a money man behind King's murder. A car bomb had silenced him forever, and smart money said no one else from the Gateway City's Mafia would feel like blabbing now.

"Could've been worse," Gantt muttered to himself, secure inside his office with the door closed. "Could've been *a lot* worse."

————

BIRMINGHAM, *Alabama: June 8, 1979*

"AT LEAST WE'VE heard the last of him," said Fee O'Hara. "Finally."

Dave Jordan didn't have to ask which "he" she had in mind. A copy of the *Birmingham Post* lay on his coffee table, open to the article describing Asa Carter's death.

Dave had no answer for Fiona, couldn't bring himself to say she should have sympathy for Carter or his family after the grief the alcoholic Klansman turned popular novelist had caused across the South during his salad days of 1955 through 1962.

"Reap what you sow, I guess," was all Jordan could manage.

Still, it was ironic. Carter, having failed to recreate

himself as an American Indian, was still using the name he'd borrowed from the KKK's first "wizard" to advance himself in literary circles. His novel *The Education of Little Tree* had been exposed as a hoax but still garnered critical raves, and he'd been working on a sequel to it—called *The Wanderings of Little Tree*—along with a screenplay for a sequel to his 1976 box office hit *The Outlaw Josey Wales*. In fact, he'd been on his way to Hollywood for a pitch session, driving cross-country from Florida, when he'd stopped off in Abilene, Texas, to visit one of the estranged sons he'd lately dubbed "nephews." Ace had shown up drunk, started a fight, fell and hit his head, then choked on his own vomit.

In Dave's view, justice didn't get much more poetic than that.

But looking at Fiona now, he knew the death that really troubled her was her brother Nolan's, murdered by a gunman still at large, while helping out the House Select Committee on Assassinations. She'd taken it hard, as expected, piled atop their father's death in a Washington car crash, and Jordan didn't have a clue how he could help her bear that load of grief.

He finally managed to ask, "You want to go out for some dinner? Maybe get some comfort food?"

"Comfort sounds good," she said, and showed him just the shadow of a smile.

———

FBI FIELD OFFICE, Manhattan: August 10, 1979

ERIN O'HARA DOUBLE-CHECKED the black armband around

her jacket sleeve before she locked her car and entered the Jacob K. Javits Federal Office Building on Foley Square. The Bureau was officially in mourning for three agents down, and while she'd never met them, Erin knew what was expected of a team player.

Special Agent Johnnie Oliver—not "John"—had nearly eight years on the job when he'd gone out yesterday with five other G-men to arrest Melvin Bay Guyon, a "Top Ten" fugitive rapist and robber, in Cleveland. Using his own infant child as a shield, Guyon managed to kill Oliver and still survive his capture by some miracle. Barely an hour later and 2,300 miles away, demented anti-government crackpot James Moloney entered the Bureau's resident agency in El Centro, California, gunning down Agents Charles Elmore and Jared Porter before he did the world a favor and committed suicide.

The murders were a shock, but Erin had grown used to that. She'd hardly been surprised this year when the U.S. prison population hit 300,000, a 33-percent jump in ten years. The gloom set in when she'd realized America hadn't hit the 200,000-prisoner mark until 1958, and before that had only recorded 100,000 inmates caged until 1927, taking 307 years from Colonial days to log the first 100,000.

What did that say about modern America, "land of the free"?

Erin tried to focus on her duties with the Bureau's Counterintelligence Division, screening reports that were mostly background noise from Afghanistan these days, but she couldn't help being distracted by Operation ABSCAM, based in NewYork but putting out feelers from D.C. to Miami. So far, she knew from interoffice memos that the sting operation led by Assistant Director Neil Welch had paid out some $400,000 in faux bribes to thirty-odd corrupt politicians, including seven members of Congress. When the bribery and conspiracy charges finally went to court, the hammer would fall on at least one senator, six congressmen, one Immigration and Naturalization Service inspector, three Philadelphia city councilmen, and the mayor of Camden, New Jersey.

And that haul, she had to admit, was barely scratching the surface of rampant corruption.

As for catching spies, the only ones she'd caught a whiff of so far came from Langley, CIA spooks eyebrow-deep in their latest not-so-secret war abroad, arming Russia's Muslim opponents in Afghanistan.

That might be official policy under President Carter, but Erin had seen enough by now to worry that American largesse might turn around someday to bite her country in the ass.

———

LITTLE ITALY, Manhattan: October 13, 1979

DEATH WAS in the air these days, and Dominic Giordano felt it wearing him down.

Johnny Dioguardi was the first to drop, in January, locked up in Pennsylvania on his latest beef for stock fraud. Closer to home, natural death for wiseguys was a rarity, with Roy DeMeo's crew from the Gambino Family running amok, murdering anyone who rubbed them the wrong way. February saw suspected stoolies Peter Waring and Freddie Todaro snuffed out in Brooklyn. March had claimed five dismembered victims, including a father and son, plus two stiffs still unidentified. Two more went down in April, one a Genovese Family *capo*, the other a college kid DeMeo mistook for a Colombian hitman. Another Gambino loyalist got the chop in May, for robbing and killing an actual Colombian without *Don* Paul Castellano's permission. In October, Roy knocked off Gambino members James Eppolito, son James Jr., and two legitimate used-car dealers who'd threatened to squeal on DeMeo's auto theft ring.

Still, the big news in Gotham murders was July's hit on Bonanno Family boss Carmine Galante and *capo* Leonardo Coppola, blasted with shotguns while dining *al fresco* at an Italian restaurant on Brooklyn's Knickerbocker Avenue. Rumor had it the contract came from Carmine's own subordinates, tired of Galante's erractic mood swings and his reliance on Old Country "zips" who could barely speak English, much less pull a hit without slaughtering innocent bystanders. Photos of Galante, blood-spattered, still clutching the trademark cigar in his teeth, had flashed worldwide overnight.

Ironically, Dom had suffered his own near-miss with death just twenty-four hours prior to Galante's assassination. That had been in Miami, on a coke-buying mission, when he'd stopped in at the stylish Dadeland Mall to pick up presents for a couple of his girlfriends. He was just stepping out of Victoria's Secret withsome lingerie bags when the shooting started, two imported Colombian shooters blazing away with machine guns, killing two targets at a nearby liquor store. Some local cop had mentioned "cocaine cowboys" on TV and now it was the hottest topic among network talking heads.

So what?

Dom had barely smelled the gunpowder that afternoon, but he knew one thing for damned sure: the drugs flowing in bulk from Medellín were worth more than their weight in gold.

———

San Salvador: October 16, 1979

THE U.S. EMBASSY in San Salvador stands on Bulevar Santa Elena, west of Madre Selva Park. As Agent Hardy Gantt passed through its gates onto the street, past two Marine Corps sentries, he reflected that he grandfather had never come this far back in the day, when he'd been sidelined from the FBI's Special Intelligence Service during the last World War. Regret over that failure nagged him till his dying day, an opportunity forever lost.

Now, gazing up and down the boulevard, Hardy decided that his grandpa hadn't missed much, after all.

El Salvador had plunged into an all-out civil war that threatened to drag on for years, if not decades. Yesterday, a self-styled Revolutionary Government Junta had deposed President Carlos Romero, driving him into Guatemalan exile. The nation's new rulers took their cue —and their cash—from Langley, with assists from Chile's DINA and the Argentine Anticommunist Alliance to field a military force they called the "Group of 14" against rebels from the Farabundo Martí National Liberation Front (FMLN). Documented government killings had hit 1,796 for the year, prompting protests even from the mostly-conservative Catholic Church. Archbishop Óscar Romero had taken his case to Washington, with a personal letter to President Carter, and now the contract on Romero's life was an open secret nationwide.

Justice of a sort had found some of Orlando Letelier's killers in January, when protected witness Michael Townley testified in Washington against assassins Alvin Diaz and the Novo Sampol brothers, Guillermo and Ignacio. Jurors convicted all three of murder, resulting in life terms for Diaz and Guillermo Sampol, while Ignacio got off with eight years. Indicted suspects Virgilio Paz and Dionisio Suarez remained at large, and the three convicted defendants were all appealing their verdicts, while no one laid a finger on General Pinochet.

As that was going on, the Sandinista National Liberation Front had finally deposed the Somoza family's hereditary dictatorship in Nicaragua, forcing President Anastasio Somoza DeBayle's flight to friendly Paraguay with Marxist assassins hot on his trail. That didn't mean the CIA was giving up, of course. Behind the scenes, Langley was shipping arms and cash to a collection of right-wing terrorists known collectively as "Contras"— literally "those against"—chiefly ex-members of Somoza's National Guard. So far, they specialized in torturing and murdering civilians, but were hoping to pull off some major-league assassinations before long.

A minor blip on the Agency's radar was pilot Barry Seal, a Green Beret wannabe who'd never finished Special Forces training but had learned to fly, employed by TWA until police caught him smuggling explosives to Mexico aboard one of the airline's DC-4s in 1972. Prosecutorial misconduct got that case thrown out two years later, and Seal went to work for Pablo Escobar's Medellín Cartel, busted again this year in Honduras. He'd saved himself from that rap by turning informer for the DEA and CIA, earning himself another get-out-of-jail-free card.

Overall, Latin American events made Southeast Asia seem tame by comparison, even though Vietnamese troops had captured Phnom Penh, ending the Khmer Rouge regime of mass murder. Would anything improve under the new masters?

Hardy had to laugh at that, experienced enough by now to know that any changes for the better in this world were few and very far between.

———

HARLEM: November 3, 1979

JUST WHEN NYPD SERGEANT PAYTON SAWYER thought he'd outgrown his capacity for being shocked, life tossed something his way that changed his mind.

He'd been mildly surprised when a white federal judge in Chicago had reinstated the wrongful death lawsuit filed against twenty-four cops and prosecutors in the 1969 murders of Black Panthers Fred Hampton and Mark Clark, finding that the state's attorney hid relevant documents and thus obstructed justice. Payton's brother had also died in that raid, but he hadn't joined the legal action, telling all who'd asked that he refused to profit from his sibling's death.

The *real* shocks, though—and there'd been two of them—had come from survivors of the Black Liberation Army and some white hangers-on from the M19 Communist Organization, calling themselves "The Family." They'd robbed a Bamberger's department store of $105,000 and used the loot to finance a pair of high-profile prison breaks, freeing dangerous radical prisoners.

The first to slip out was William Morales, raised in East Harlem, a bomb-maker for the militant Puerto Rican separatist group FALN, whose name translated from Spanish to Armed Forces of National Liberation. One of his bombs had wrecked Manhattan's historic Fraunces Tavern in January 1975, killing four victims and wounding more than fifty others. Another bomb had maimed him three years later, costing Morales one eye and nine fingers, giving him the nickname "No Hands." Arrested at the scene, he'd been tried in February of this year, convicted not of murder, but for possessing and transporting explosives. On May 21st, members of The Family helped him escape from Bellevue Hospital on First Avenue. From there, No Hands had made his way to Mexico and was incarcerated there for now, pleading for Cuban asylum. In the wake of his flight, the Powers That Be had fired New York City Department of Correction Commissioner William Ciuros Jr. and fifteen others, charged with incompetence.

Sawyer hadn't known whether to laugh or snarl at that, but the next jailbreak left him seething. On November 2nd, three men and one woman—calling themselves the "BLA Multinational Task Force," although the female was white—had turned up at Jersey's Clinton Correctional Facility for Women, taking two guards hostage and springing JoAnneChesimard, aka "Assata Shakur" and "Soul of the BLA," before they fled in a van, dropping the guards unharmed in a nearby parking lot.

Sheepish prison officials admitted that they hadn't checked the raiders' fake IDs or searched them for weapons before they'd reached the visiting room. More heads would roll, Payton supposed, but what good did that do with Chesimard in the wind, presumably bound for exile in Havana? When the FBI papered Gotham with her WANTED posters, supporters countered with posters reading "Assata Shakur is Welcome Here," and a National Black Human Rights Coalition had rallied some 5,000 marchers demanding a free, independent "New Afrikan state."

So far, the feds had identified two members of the raiding party: BLA veteran Jeral Williams, aka "Mutulu Shaku," and Weatherman prison escapee Marilyn Buck. Hoping it would help, their names were added to the Bureau's "Most Wanted" list, beside radical fugitives Raymond Levasseur, Carlos Morales, and Katherine Power.

Sawyer didn't like the FBI's chances of recapturing Chesimard or Morales, but he supposed other BLA members might resurface now that they'd returned to action after years in hiding. And when they did, he guessed, the net result would be hell in a handbasket.

───────

EVANSTON, Illinois: November 20, 1979

WHOEVER SAID lightning never strikes twice in the same place was wrong. Special Agent Wyman Gantt knew that for sure. Why else would he be back at Northwestern University, seeking clues to identify a terrorist at large that Bureau headquarters had tagged the "Unabomber"?

The nickname came from Bureau-speak that had labeled the case "UNABOM," short for "*un*iversity and *a*irline *bom*ber." The phantom's second device, like the first, had detonated on Northwestern's campus, inflicting minor cuts and burns on a graduate student who claimed he didn't have an enemy in the world. That was back on May 9th, but five days ago a third bomb had exploded aboard American Airlines Flight 444, en route from Chicago to Washington, D.C. Dumb luck or crafty planning had averted disaster, sparing seventy-eight passengers and six crew members from a fiery death. Experts opined that the bomb, carried in the jet's cargo hold, had caused "a sucking explosion and a loss of pressure," leaving a dozen passengers discomfited by minor smoke inhalation.

The result so far: no leads to the bomber, but creation of a Bureau-led task force including helpers from the U.S. Postal Inspection Service and Treasury's Bureau of Alcohol, Tobacco, and Firearms. So far, Wyman hadn't been conscripted for that group effort, but when he was, he hoped the ATF gang brought along some of their alcohol.

The whole team was likely to need it.

So, he guessed, might the former Bureau leaders facing trial in New York City for their countless COIN-TELPRO crimes. Patrick Gray had lost his bid to dismiss the charges based on "lack of personal jurisdiction," pleading that he didn't know about and hadn't ordered any of the felonies committed by various G-men during his eleven months as Bureau Director, claiming—unlike Harry Truman—that no bucks ever stopped with him except the paycheck he'd received monthly.

While that nonsense went down the toilet, codefendants Mark Felt and Edward Miller tried to cut a plea deal with Justice, offering guilty pleas to misdemeanor counts of conducting searches without lawful warrants. That had been a hoot, two former top men with the Bureau claiming that they didn't know the basic Bill of Rights, and those bids to escape meaningful punishment had been laughed out of courts.

Gantt sympathized with them, to some extent, but what the hell? Why should the men who'd been in charge believe they were immune from prosecution while the agents who had served them wouldn't be?

Forget about "Fidelity, Bravery, Integrity," Gantt thought. Whenever someone raised the rock and saw what lived beneath it, it would always be a case of each man for himself.

———

FBI HEADQUARTERS: November 27, 1979

TUESDAY AFTER THANKSGIVING, and Special Agent Devon Gantt felt like he ought to hit the gym this afternoon, but he was too damned tired. That's what he got for being fifty-seven, with the better part of four decades in service to the Bureau, and no matter how he looked at it, it was too late to turn his life around and start afresh.

Gantt and his wife Eileen had hosted their son Wyman for the holiday and heard about his work on the case headquarters was calling UNABOM. Another crackpot terrorist at large, as if there weren't enough of them already, and so far the Bureau didn't have a clue to his or her identity, much less a motive for the crimes. The bastard hadn't murdered anybody yet, but every time he mailed another bomb the odds of death or permanent disfigurement increased.

For Devon's part, his orders were to keep on watching groups and individuals he had been stalking since the good old COINTELPRO years, but keep it on the downlow and avoid the tactics now forbidden since the Church Committee had revealed excesses by the FBI, the CIA and NSA.

No sweat. Most of the folks he was investigating had a penchant for creating media headlines.

Take Huey Newton, founder of the once-fearsome Black Panther Party. After time abroad in Africa, Cuba and China—which he'd called a "free and liberated territory"—Newton had returned to Oakland. He'd been acquitted of punching his tailor in 1974, while two successive juries deadlocked over charges that he'd killed a prostitute that same year. More recently, in August, he'd been shot and killed by a parolee who was claiming self-defence against one count of first-degree murder.

Another goner, only yesterday, was Fleeta Drumgo, twice acquitted of killing prison guards, paroled from his original burglary conviction in 1976 to share digs in L.A. with fellow "Soledad Brother" John Clutchette. Just yesterday, two unknown men had gunned him down and fled the scene.

Fay Stender, a onetime Soledad Brothers defense attorney, had been luckier in May, surviving five gunshots from paroled Black Guerrilla Family member Edward Brooks, after he forced her to write a note saying, "I, Fay Stender, admit I betrayed George Jackson and the prison movement when they needed me most." Police nabbed Brooks in mid-June, robbing a bank, and matched his pistol to the slugs retrieved from Fender. They also suspected him in Drumgo's murder but were short on evidence.

Two months after the bungled bank heist, still in L.A., BGF member and crack cocaine dealer Elrader Browning murdered victims Aubrey Harris and Luellen Thomas. Police claimed he'd acted under orders from BGF "Supreme Commander" John "Doc" Holiday, but they hadn't proved it yet.

Another one to watch was Hulon Mitchell Jr., aka "Yahweh ben Yaweh," founder and overlord of a new religion dubbed the Nation of Yahweh. Mitchell's father was a minister in Oklahoma, where his mother played piano during services, but Junior wanted something more in line with his personal narcissism. Moving to Miaimi's Liberty City ghetto this year, he'd founded his own cult, denouncing whites in general and Jews in particular as "infidels and oppressors." He hadn't crossed the line into crime yet, but was flirting with it, demanding that his followers revere him as the son of God.

Meanwhile, the news for AIM activist and convicted G-man killer Leonard Peltier was all bad. In July he'd joined two other inmates in an effort to escape from Lompoc, California's federal lockup. Guards had killed one of the runners, and another was recaptured ninety minutes later, but Peltier remained at large for three days, caught after robbing a farmer near Santa Maria in Santa Barbara County. He'd been packing an M14 rifle when found, but offered no resistance to arrest, so the manhunters had no excuse to finish him.

And maybe it was better that way, Devon mused. Let him rot in prison, now with more time added to his two life sentences, while wishing he was safe and sound, back on the reservation after all.

FBI FIELD OFFICE, Manhattan: December 28, 1979

ALL THE BUREAU news these days seemed to involve Afghanistan, and while his KGB controller didn't seem to mind, Agent Stephen Barnes kept hoping for a case that hit closer to home, involving Russian spies he could assist by leaking crucial Bureau documents.

How better to pursue his father's work of bringing disrepute and ruin to the FBI?

A year had passed since Afghanistan's communist government invited Soviet troops and tanks to police the country, but violence by Muslim mujahideen rebels had only increased, supported by the CIA. Langley called its meddling "Operation Cyclone," funneling arms and cash to tribal warlords while Western observers branded government leader Hafizullah Amin a "butal psychopath" in media reports. Soviet Chairman Leonid Brezhnev had signed SALT II strategic arms limitations with President Carter in June, but when he tried to relieve some of the pressure in Afghanistan he'd chosen a strange way to do so.

From the original "invitation" for military aid, Amin's regime had escalated to requests for Mil Mi-24 helicopter gunships—"Hinds" in NATO parlance—plus ever-increasing numbers of troops and armored vehicles. Yesterday, 700 Red Army troops clad in Afghan uniforms, trailed by KGB agents, had occupied major governmental, military and media buildings in Kabul, including the Tajbeg Presidential Palace, where they executed President Amin. All were secured by this morning, when 80,000 soldiers, 1,800 tanks, and 2,000 smaller armored fighting vehicles invaded from the north, intent on crushing Sunni guerillas and any other source of serious dissent.

The down side: foreign ministers from various Islamic nations had voiced instant outrage over the invasion, and now some Western pundits were claiming that Russian détente with America was "already effectively dead."

Barnes greeted that as music to his ears, coupled with seizure of the U.S. embassy in Teheran by Islamic militants, holding fifty-two hostages. One of those was America's Chargé d'Affaires Bruce Laingen, although Ambassador William Sullivan and six other diplomats managed to slip through the net. Barnes regretted that no Bureau agents were among the prisoners, further exacerbating strain at headquarters, but he would take what he could get.

Tonight, again, he would be working overtime and snapping photos of selected files with the Minox Riga subminiature camera concealed in a secret compartment of his hand-tooled briefcase. With any luck, some of the documents would help Moscow uncover U.S. agents working in Russia or elsewhere in the Eastern Bloc.

The only difficulty Barnes faced was concealing his activities from prying eyes within his own Bureau division, taking special care with Agent Erin O'Hara. He mistrusted her casual overtures of friendship, constantly alert for treachery.

And who knew better than he did, the darkness lurking in the hearts of his purported fellow patriots?

CHAPTER 7

COLBY GANTT SUPPOSED it was the Agency's finest hour, deception without any trace of mayhem, and he'd been left out of it.

No problem. Even as a hoary veteran he clearly recognized that younger minds were rising to control his world.

Back in November, while the U.S. ambassador escaped Teheran, six of his subordinates had managed to reach the Canadian embassy unobserved. Langley had hatched a plot with Canadian Prime Minister Joe Clark and Secretary of State for External Affairs Flora MacDonald, inserting CIA disguise and exfiltration expert Tony Mendez as a supposed South American filmmaker enamored of Iran's revolution, working on a nonexistent documentary called *Argo*. Once in Iran, Mendez had visited the Canadian embassy—still unmolested by rioting Shia radicals calling themselves "students"—and distributed false passports issued from Ottawa to his six newfound "assistants."

Blinded by fanatic hatred of America alone, no radicals saw through the phony film crew as it moved around Tehran, finally departing from Mehrabad Airport yesterday, aboard a Swissair flight to Zurich, and from there back home. After debriefings by the Agency, the six escapees were reunited with their families and all was well.

When Gantt looked back across his thirty-eight years as a CIA agent—toppling lawful governments on three continents, assassinating foreign leaders (or failing to), subverting popular revolutions for the benefit of U.S. industry—he seldom felt conflicted about anything he'd done. He was his father's son, born to the creeds of anticommunism and containment, doing anything to save democracy as his superiors envisioned it, including the elimination of dynamic politicians on the homefront.

All of that was fine with Colby, and he'd long since made his peace with it.

But this time was the first, even as an observer on the sidelines, that he had felt *proud*.

And that, he thought, entitled him to knock off early for a drink or three.

HARLEM: July 4, 1980

NYPD SERGEANT PAYTON SAWYER listened to sporadic fireworks in the street outside and hoped that all the noise was made by firecrackers, not guns. In Harlem these days, with the rise of crack cocaine, it could go either way.

In Chicago's federal court, where surviving relatives of two Black Panthers murdered by police were still pressing their claim against the Cook County's state's attorney and the cops who'd done the killing, declassified FBI reports proved that victim Fred Hampton had lived and died under constant illegal Bureau harassment, along with onetime Panther Party "Minister of Defense" Rap Brown, lately known to fans as "Jamil Abdullah Al-Amin." That might sway a jury, Sawyer supposed, but it mainly turned his thoughts toward Brown and how the former black militant leader had changed over time.

Paroled from Attica four years ago, Brown/Al-Amin had moved to Georgia, opened a grocery store in Atlanta, and converted to Islam, preaching against drugs and gambling in the city's West End. He'd joined the Dar al-Islam movement, based at Brooklyn's State Street Mosque, but that had lately changed with a split at movement headquarters that left him momentarily leaderless.

Another Muslim name-changer, ex-Black Panther Muhammad Ali Hassan, born Albert Dickens, had been released last month after serving sixteen years in New Jersey, but prison hadn't reformed him. Almost before he could appreciate freedom, He'd loaned his car, fitted with stolen plates, to five New World of Islam members for a bank heist in New Brunswick. Dickens and fifteen NWI codefendants had refused to participate in their trial, which made it easy for the state to lock them up on RICO conspiracy charges.

The one who got away remained JoAnne Chesimard, purported "den mother" and "soul" of the Black Liberation Army. Still at large eight months after her jailbreak in

Jersey, Chesimard was a major thorn in the FBI's side. Director William Webster publicly complained that non-cooperation from New Yorkers kept G-men from catching Chesimard, while the *New York Times* chastized the Bureau for its "apparently crude sweep" through Harlem, sniffing for clues. Rumored sightings placed the fugitive in Upper Manhattan, walking her daughter to school, or possibly in Philadelphia.

If it was me, thought Sawyer, *I'd have left the States by now.*

Or maybe that was just him, on the shady side of fifty now and wishing he could take off for the tropics—hell, go anywhere and leave his cover life with BOSS behind.

——————

MANHATTAN: October 4, 1980

LEAVING HIS SECRET MAIL DROP, Special Agent Stephen Barnes took all the usual precautions to detect watchers along the route of travel that would take him to the nearest subway station for his journey home.

No one was waiting for him at his small, austere apartment where he lived alone and rarely welcomed visitors. He spotted no one on his tail, but stayed alert while letting part of his mind drift away to Moscow, unacknowledged city of his birth, and to Afghanistan, where Russian troops were presently engaged in what appeared to be a hopeless war.

Dissent against that war had reared its head at home, prompting internal exile of Andrei Sakharov, renowned nuclear physicist and 1975 Nobel Peace Prize winner, now confined to Gorki Leninskiye, a city six miles south of Moscow that was closed to foreigners. A month later, Washington had announced plans to boycott the Summer Olympic Games, scheduled to proceed at great expense in Moscow, opening in mid-July. That embarrassment, together with legalization of the new trade union Solidarity, devoted to civil resistance inside the People's Republic of Poland, left the Kremlin looking somewhat weak and foolish.

Not that anyone in Moscow seemed to give a damn. While CIA headquarters armed and bankrolled mujahideen "freedom fighters"—in truth, Muslim fanatics who might just as happily make war against America— the Red Army pressed one offensive after another in strategically critical Panjshir Province, northeast of Kabul, while most foreign observers agreed that guerilla warlords controlled up to 80 percent of the Afghan countryside.

Britain had learned that lesson to its ultimate sorrow, waging three successive Afghan wars between 1839 and 1919, but Russia's leaders—like America's—somehow managed to ignore lessons from history, convinced that they could do it better, get it right, if only they tried harder, making more and more determined enemies. Extensive depopulation campaigns in eleven of Afghanistan's thirty-four provinces only hardened resistance, as did criminal incidents such as the Soviet gang rapes of women kidnapped for "interrogation" from Darul Aman, Kama, Khair Khana, Laghman—even Kabul itself. Dismissing history, it seemed that fools would never learn even from their immediate mistakes, simply repeat them in displays of arrogance that ultimately led to their destruction.

Barnes, for his part, couldn't have cared less what happened in Afghanistan or any other distant hot spot on the planet. He'd been raised from childhood to achieve one goal: humiliation of the FBI that had abused his biological father and twice deported him from the purported Land of Opportunity to Mother Russia.

Barnes was on his way to reaching that goal now, though it would not be swift or easy to destroy the Bureau, an American icon despite all its faults, established in the distant past preceding Russia's revolution and invention of the Model T.

Not easy, no. But he had pledged his life to it, and nothing short of death would alter that.

———

FBI HEADQUARTERS: October 13, 1980

NO MATTER how you rolled the cosmic dice, then always seemed to come up snakeyes for America's minority and left-wing radicals. How else would Special Agent Devon Gantt still have a job and still be tracking enemies he'd hunted in the COINTELPRO years that now embarrassed most officials who'd survived them in the nation's capital?

It troubled Gantt that some subversives from those bygone days were making good now, after causing so much chaos. In Los Angeles, ex-convict and ex-FBI informer Ron "Maulana" Karenga was working on his second doctorate, still peddling Kwanzaa as an authentic African religion that he'd suddenly discovered back in 1966. Another survivor—Richard Henry, aka "Imari Abubakari Obadele," formerly a Republic of New Afrika leader—had done his Mississippi prison time and recently earned his Ph.D. in political science from Temple University, simultaneously filing a $2.4 million lawsuit against COINTELPRO agents who'd surveilled and harassed him.

Good luck with that, Gantt thought, his mind turning to Black Liberation Army member Russell "Maroon" Shoatz, convicted of killing a cop in 1972, lately escaped from Pennsylvania's maximum-security lockup at Waymart after clumsy guards missed smuggled firearms. A lot of good it did him, free for just three days before he was recaptured by state police.

Another militant in the loser category was Edward Brooks, convicted and sentenced to prison for last year's attempted murder of former radical lawyer Fay Stender. If Brooks kept his nose clean, he should hit the streets again in 1997.

Meanwhile, new groups kept emerging, demanding the Bureau's urgent attention. Two presently in Devon's sights were Earth First!, founded in April by radical environmentalists, and CISPES—the Committee in Solidarity with the People of El Salvador—launched in October to oppose America's latest covert war abroad.

Earth First! claimed to take its cue from environmental writing such as Rachel Carson's *Silent Spring,* welcoming a few ex-Yippies to its activist "Monkey Wrench Gang." So far, that team had limited its protests to political "theater" like their stunt unfurling a long plastic "crack" on Arizona's Glen Canyon Dam, but Gantt detected a potential threat in their motto "No compromise in defense of Mother Earth!" What did that mean, and how far would they go? So far, no one would say.

CISPES, by contrast, was clearly subversive by FBI standards, opposing America's funding of El Salvador's right-wing. In the old days, under Hoover, agents would've been wiretapping, stealing mail and burgling offices, spreading dissension via fabricated letters and bad-jacketing of CISPES loyalists as informers, but those tactics weren't allowed today.

Or were they?

Gantt personally knew of G-men who had exceeded their authority, ignoring guidelines recently imposed upon them by alleged superiors at Justice, and it almost seemed to Devon that the old ways were about to make a comeback.

And why not? They might have been illegal, but at least they mostly worked.

BIRMINGHAM, Alabama: November 4, 1980

"HE'S WINNING, DAMMIT!" Fiona O'Hara sounded furious. "Can you believe it?"

"Sure," Dave Jordan said, "with the campaign he's run."

"Just look at him," Fee said, pointing a rigid index finger toward Dave's television set. "He's sixty-eight and wrinkled as a prune, but claims he doesn't dye his hair. I mean, just listen to him read his speeches. I can't be the only one who thinks he's senile."

"The voters seem to disagree with you," Dave said.

"You mean the *sheep*."

But numbers didn't lie—at least, not this time. Ronald Reagan, former far-right governor of California after a lackluster Hollywood career, had buried Democratic incumbent Jimmy Carter to become America's next president, sweeping forty-four states and 489 votes in the Electoral College. Of course, it didn't hurt that he'd allied himself with the Bible-thumping "Moral Majority" and the corrupt Teamsters Union, naming mobbed-up Cleveland Teamster leader Jackie Presser, an eighth-grade dropout, as Reagan's top labor advisor.

But it was Reagan's barely-hidden racism, doubling down on Nixon's old "southern strategy," that turned Dave's stomach worst of all. It was clearly no mistake that Reagan had delivered his first campaign speech on August 3rd at Mississippi's Neshoba County Fair, seven miles from the site where three civil rights workers were murdered by Klansmen in June 1964. His topic was "states' rights"—the same old dog whistle blown by Dixie racists from secession to their modern fight for segregation—vowing to "restore to states and local governments the power that properly belongs to them."

And any fool who believed that was clearly dumb enough to pick a has-been actor as the country's Chief Executive.

As it was, 15,000 fans had turned out to the event, sponsored by congressman Trent Lott, from whose fraternity U.S. Marshals had seized weapons during the 1962 racist riots at Ole Miss. They'd hooted and hollered as Reagan "reminded" them of a myth he'd just concocted—that the Ku Klux Klan was supposedly "born in Indiana," rather than in Tennessee.

Business as usual in presidential politics.

Dave wondered how the Gipper's southern fans would like it when he started making economic raids on Medicare and Social Security, two programs despised by

Republican leaders since their inception, utilized more widely in Dixie than in most other parts of the nation.

Finally, he let it go, thinking, *You get the government you vote for. And how's that for "Love It or Leave It?"*

———

FBI FIELD OFFICE, Manhattan: November 8, 1980

ERIN O'HARA SCANNED the latest field reports from FBI legal attachés at U.S. embassies in Turkey, Israel and India for updates on Russia's invasion of Afghanistan, but it was difficult for her to block out thoughts of Operation ABSCAM, finally producing criminal indictments.

The biggest fish they'd hooked, so far, was Senator Harrison Williams of New Jersey, charged with nine counts of bribery and conspiracy to use his office in aid of business ventures, including a fictional titanium mine. Another Jersey catch was Congressman Frank Thompson, charged with taking bribes from the Bureau's phony "Arab sheik" to help other mythical Arabs dodge American immigration restrictions. True to his fellow crooks, if not his oath of office, Thompson had abstained from the House vote to expel Representative Michael Myers of Pennsylvania. Another Pennsylvania congressman, John Murtha, had refused a $50,000 bribe on camera but steered Bureau sting operators toward Thompson and New York's John Murphy, another lawmaker now under indictment.

Another Jerseyite who took $10,000, State Senator Joseph Maressa, was trying to whitewash the bribe by telling reporters, "I felt like it would be patriotic to take some of this OPEC oil money and get it back to the United States." For reasons Erin couldn't understand, Justice had chosen not to prosecute him for the crime they caught on videotape.

Now, no surprise, Congress had embarked upon an investigation of FBI undercover techniques via the House Subcommittee on Civil and Constitutional Rights. They'd never admit it, of course, but to Erin it smelled like payback for ABSCAM, and what else was new? At its beginning, back in 1908, the Bureau was only created after federal legislators nabbed for dirty dealings banned further "loans" of U.S. Secret Service agents to the Justice Department.

Glancing up from her paperwork, Erin saw Agent Stephen Barnes bearing an armload of files toward his desk and raised a hand in greetings. He nodded in reply but seemed distracted, which appeared to be his normal state.

Not for the first time, Erin wondered what was going on inside his head and why, against all logic, simply looking at him seemed to set her teeth on edge.

———

SAN SALVADOR: *December 3, 1980*

HARDY GANTT AVOIDED visits to the U.S. Embassy whenever he could manage it, and then often adopted a disguise. He took for granted that the FMLN had the embassy under surveillance, prompting him to travel armed at all times, as he had in Southeast Asia, as a hedge against kidnapping or assassination.

In the States, protests were mounting against U.S. meddling in the country's civil war, particularly when it came down on the side of government brutality and murder. A group called Human Rights Watch had reported that the embassy "apparently collaborated" with right-wing death squads, briefly confining two law students kidnapped in January, who were whisked away and never seen again. The embassy denied it, naturally, but so what? Catholic Archbishop Óscar Romero's February assassination came shortly after he'd penned a letter to President Carter, protesting American support for the Revolutionary Government Junta, and CIA memos admitted support for the far-right Atlacatl Battalion, trained at the U.S. Army's School of the Americas in Panama.

Only yesterday, soldiers of the Salvadoran National Guard had been named as prime suspects in the gang-rape and murder of four American nuns and a female traveling companion. The outgoing Carter administration's response: $10 million more in aid to the junta, half of that earmarked for helicopters and weapons, the rest tagged "humanitarian aid."

Back home, meanwhile, as Hardy had predicted, an appellate court had overturned the guilty verdicts of Orlando Letelier's convicted killers, freeing two, while bomber Guillermo Novo Sampol still faced fifty-four months for lying to a grand jury.

In June, Langley was forewarned of Bolivia's impending "cocaine coup," financed by drug traffickers and supported by European mercenaries whose recruiter —Klaus Barbie, former Gestapo "Butcher of Lyons" in France—was one of the Agency's pet Nazis. Despite that warning, the CIA kept quiet and sat on its hands in mid-

July, when General Luis García Meza deposed Bolivia's first female president, Lidia Gueiler Tejada, and imposed police state rule rivaling Chile's record for torture and murder. Net result: cocaine imports by the U.S. were swiftly rising, earning traffickers an estimated $850 million so far.

Sometime CIA pilot Barry Seal was in the thick of it all, fresh out of prison and banking an average $1.3 million per flight to his home base in Louisiana, lately shifted to Mena Intermountain Municipal Airport in Polk County, Arkansas. He was greasing cops and politicians from the county seat to Little Rock, selling airplanes as a cover for his sudden flood of cash.

Peru, meanwhile, had joined the Operation Condor club in June, collaborating with Argentina's 601 Intelligence Battalion to murder exiled leftist Montoneros living in Lima, but the abuse of human rights had grown too flagrant for Peruvians to stomach. They'd rebelled against dictator Francisco Morales-Bermúdez in late July, demanding that he keep his promise to restore democracy after five years of autocratic rule. Now, exiled President Fernando Belaúnde was back from teaching at various American universities, swiftly restoring silenced newspapers to their rightful owners and grappling with the economy Morales-Bermúdez had nearly bankrupted.

Surveying Latin America, Gantt saw little hope for positive change in most countries so far, and that was fine. Langley was paying him to keep the status quo in place and undisturbed, until some fat cats stateside reckoned it was time for yet another coup to beef up their off-shore accounts, all in the name of fighting communism.

———

MANHATTAN: December 4, 1980

THE VIOLENT NEW Left might not be dead, but it was tottering, and Special Agent Wyman Gantt would take what he could get.

Weather Underground fugitive Cathy Wilkerson had surrendered to NYPD in August, drawing a three-year sentence on charges related to the 1970 Greenwich Village townhouse explosion, but local courts went easier on others. David Gilbert had sired a son with lover Kathy Boudin, the baby born in August, but Boudin and child remained in hiding when Gilbert and colleague Bernardine Dohrn presented themselves for arrest in New York. Ayers's pending charges were dropped due to illegal Bureau wiretaps and other COINTELPRO crimes, while Dohrn got off with three years' probation and a $15,000 fine.

Meanwhile, the Unabomber had resurfaced in June, mailing an explosive parcel to Percy Wood, president of United Airlines, at his home in Evanston, Illinois. The package, marked "book rate," arrived one week after Wood got a letter telling him he'd been listed to receive a free copy of Sloan Wilson's novel *Ice Brothers*, about Coast Guardsmen patrolling Greenland's shores in World War Two. The book came hollowed out, a bomb hidden inside, but Wood survived the blast while suffering extensive cuts and burns. Forensic analysts found the letters "FC" hand-etched into the pipe bomb but couldn't interpret them. A typewritten note enclosed with the novel told Wood, "You will find it of great social significance."

After that, the Bureau's Behavioral Sciences Unit profiled their unknown subject as a man of above-average intellect, with ties to academia, but that brought street agents no closer to arresting him.

In D.C.'s federal court, after eight postponements, the COINTELPRO trial of Mark Felt and Edward Miller finally convened in September, by which time charges filed on ex-Director Patrick Gray had been dismissed. Defense witnesses included ex-President Nixon, who told the court that FDR had ordered Bureau break-ins four decades prior to Nixon's own abuses, which he still regarded as entirely legal. Tricky Dick had also anted up some cash toward Felt's legal expenses, presently topping $600,000. Former Attorneys General Herbert Brownell Jr., Nicholas Katzenbach, Ramsey Clark, John Mitchell, and Richard Kleindienst lined up to insist that warrantless break-ins were commonplace in national security cases and "not understood to be illegal," though Mitchell and Kleindienst denied approving any of the crimes charged against Felt and Miller.

Jurors didn't buy the "business as usual" defense, convicting both defendants on November 6th. Although both men faced a maximum of ten years and $10,000 fines, Judge William Bryant let them slide with virtual wrist-slaps, fining Felt $5,000 and Miller $3,500 with no prison time.

That didn't end the case, of course. In January, eight New Left COINTELPRO targets filed a civil rights complaint in New York City, naming defendants Gray, Felt and Miller; FBI Director Webster; ex-G-men John Kearney and Wallace Laprade; Richard Nixon; U.S. Postmaster General William Bolger; ex-Attorneys General Mitchell and Griffin Bell; and the New York Telephone Company that facilitated warrantless wiretaps. For good measure, the lawsuit added included an uncertain

number of "John Does," names unknown, sued "individu-
ally and as former and current agents and employees of
the FBI."

Nixon sought dismissal with the same old wheeze of
"absolute immunity from liability" at trial, quickly denied.
Gray wanted his case tossed on grounds that New York
had no jurisdiction over him (denied), and Mitchell
claimed his case was barred by the statute of limitations
(also denied, on grounds of fraudulent concealment).
Other FBI agents, named or unknown, lost their pleas for
dismissal based on "lack of specificity." Defendants Bell,
Bolger and Webster were dismissed from the case, while
Felt and Miller obtained stays pending conclusion of their
criminal trial.

The lawsuit would continue over time, but Gantt was
betting that the plaintiffs would be losers in the end, even
if they emerged victorious, while lawyers gobbled up most
of the damages awarded for their suffering.

———

LITTLE ITALY, Manhattan: December 17, 1980

"I'M sick of all this shit about El Salvador," Angelo Giordano said, switching the television from news to Home
Box Office using his remote control. "Can't no one see we
got a war right here?"

"Seeing's one thing," his brother Dominic replied.
"They just don't care."

Ange wasn't wrong, for once. A war *was* plaguing *Cosa
Nostra*—maybe even two wars at the same time, now Dom
stopped to think about it. Roy DeMeo's crew was still

dropping bodies, running a tab that would likely top out a 100 or more. Their latest, in March, was suspected stoolie Joseph Coppolino, stabbed and beheaded, dumped on a Brooklyn Street for police to discover.

Philadelphia was seeing the real action, though, the echoes audible in Gotham from ninety-five miles away. Two weeks after the Coppolino hit in Gotham, *capo crimine* Angelo Bruno, the so-called "Gentle Don," was killed by a shotgun blast in his car, his driver wounded, outside Bruno's home. Scuttlebutt blamed the hit on family *consigliere* Antonio Caponigro, who received an urgent summons from *La Commissione*. The other bosses reminded Caponigro that the Bruno hit was neither sanctioned nor desired. Caponigro turned around and blamed Genovese Family boss Frank Tieri for ordering the execution, but Tieri denied it. On April 17th, Bronx enforcer Joseph "Mad Dog" Sullivan took out Caponigro and his cousin-cauffeur Al Salerno, shooting Caponigro fourteen times before stuffing his mouth and rectum with cash to denote his fatal case of greed.

That should've ended Philly's war, with Phillip "Chicken Man" Testa succeeding Bruno as boss, but no such luck. In September *capo* John "Johnny Keys" Simone got whacked, followed in October by another *capo*, Frank "The Barracuda" Sindone. Almost as an afterthought, just yesterday, a shooter disguised as a flower deliveryman had drilled John McCullough, mobbed-up president of Roofer's Union Local 30, in his home's kitchen.

With all that going on in Philly, New York's papers almost overlooked Gerard Pappa, a onetime Colombo Family soldier who'd defected to work for the Genovese Family, sometimes dressed in drag when he carried out contracts. One target he'd tagged was Colombo Family *capo* Thomas "Shorty" Spero, missing and presumed dead since February of this year. Justice caught up with Pappa in July, when a Colombo hit team blasted him with shotguns in Brooklyn's Villa Sixty-Six Restaurant.

Better them than me, thought Dominic. And the way things were going, he figured some coked-up Colombian wingnut was as likely to kill him as anybody. That was the risk he took for moving major product on the streets, but it was like he'd grown addicted to the drug himself—not snorting it, but rolling in the cash he made from selling it to junkies around town.

God bless free enterprise.

CHAPTER 8

BIRMINGHAM, ALABAMA: MARCH 23, 1981

JUST WHEN DAVE JORDAN thought the ugly past was ready to lie down and die, it rose again and smacked him in the face.

Past fifty now and often feeling it, he could remember tales of southern lynchings from newspapers in his youth, but here and now? How could it be?

Okay, he thought. *So not right here, but close enough.*

Mobile lay some 250 miles south, on the Gulf, and that was where 'Bama's latest atrocity had recently occurred. The city had been up in arms already, with a black man on trial for killing a white cop, the jury deadlocked for a mistrial. While that was going on, a local branch of the United Klans—same bunch that killed four little girls bombing a church and murdered three white civil rights supporters in the Sixties—had decided "an example" was required to set things right. Their answer: string somebody up.

The victim, picked at random if the FBI could be believed, was nineteen-year-old Michael Donald, beaten, with his throat cut, then hanged from a tree on the same street as local Klan headquarters. Subtlety had never caught on in the Cotton State.

Police had four Klansmen in custody: the state's "Grand Klaliff"—second in command below the "Grand Dragon"—his son, and two other suspects, one just seventeen. It seemed that Mobile's D.A. would be filing murder charges, and the feds were talking about civil rights indictments for dessert, but Dave knew that could be a problem. The Assistant U.S. Attorney for Alabama's Southern District, Jefferson Sessions III, was a Reagan appointee who'd been asked for his opinion of the Klan by a reporter. If the printed article was accurate, Sessions had answered back, "Okay, until I found out they smoked pot." Now he was pulling back from that, saying his comment was "a joke," but what the hell?

Dave knew he'd have to watch this case, first for indictments at the state and federal levels, then to see if jurors would convict white men in Alabama for the same shit they'd been pulling without punishment in state courts since the Civil War.

The more he thought about it, Jordan wondered if it might not be time he went back home to New York.

———

CIA Headquarters: May 14, 1981

Sometimes it seemed to Colby Gantt that he was living in

a time warp, with a spate of 1960's-style political assassinations ramping up again.

Of course, they'd never really stopped, and during his two decades plus of service with the CIA, the Agency had been involved in many of them, from Patrice Lumumba and Ngô Đình Diệm to Salvador Allende and Orlando Letelier, not counting Kennedys. Still, so far this year, there'd been another surge of them, as if saluting President Reagan's appointment of William Casey—Gantt's acquaintance from the wartime OSS that spawned the CIA—as Director of Central Intelligence.

Whether that was good or bad remained to be seen.

Ironically, perhaps, Reagan himself had been the year's first target on March 30th, ambushed by a gunman as he left the Washington Hilton after making a speech. The would-be killer emptied his .22-caliber revolver— shades of Sirhan!—before Reagan's bodyguards swarmed him, bullets striking Reagan, White House Press Secretary James Brady, a Secret Service agent, and a D.C. cop. All survived, though Brady—the worst injured with a head wound causing permanent brain damage—was initially reported dead. Reagan was hospitalized with a broken rib and punctured lung, but he'd bounced back quickly for an old guy and was out within two weeks.

The shooting had been covered live on all three major TV networks, and before the final body count was in, Langley was already investigating triggerman John Warnock Hinckley Jr., praying that he had no links to Operation MKULTRA and had never served the Agency in any way, no matter how obscure and trivial. They'd caught a break, determining that Hinckley was a mental case, fired up after he saw the movie *Taxi Driver* five years earlier and fell in love with teenage actress Jodie Foster, cast as a hooker enslaved by Harvey Keitel portraying a pimp called "Sport." In the film's last reel, star Robert De Niro tries to shoot a presidential candidate but gets scared off, then kills Sport and his mob associates before attempting suicide and failing. The "twist" ending finds him celebrated as a hero, back driving his cab around New York at night.

Love-sick and crazy as a rabid bat, Hinckley decided to "impress" Foster by emulating De Niro's shooting spree, but sticking to a target everyone on Earth would recognize. Gantt hadn't seen the movie previously—who had time?—but watched it after Reagan's shooting, gratified that Hinckley would be locked up in a loony bin until his hair turned white and all his teeth fell out.

So much for fame.

And then, just yesterday, a Turk named Mehmet Ali Ağca had shot Pope John Paul II as the pontiff rode around St. Peter's Square in Vatican City, waving from his open Fiat Popemobile and blessing thousands of assembled Catholics who couldn't have been happier until the shots rang out. Unlike the Reagan shooting, Ağca came loaded for bear, with a 9mm Browning automatic, and hit his man four times before he was mobbed and disarmed. The pope suffered severe blood loss but physicians predicted a full recovery.

Another difference between Ağca and John Hinckley: the Turk had killed before, and he was definitely part of a conspiracy.

It hadn't taken Agency assets in Europe any time at all to flesh out details of the plot. Langley already knew that Ağca was a member of the Grey Wolves, a far-right ultra-nationalist group organized in 1968, responsible for a series of massacres that killed 286 people and wounded hundreds more between 1977 and '80. Ağca, acting alone, had murdered leftist newspaper editor Abdi İpekçi in Istanbul, in February 1979.

According to the intel reaching Gantt, the papal plot was hatched in August 1980, by Bekir Çelenk—a Turkish mobster hiding in Bulgaria—and overseen by Zilo Vassilev, the Bulgarian military attaché in Italy. The Grey Wolves accepted Çelenk's offer—equivalent to $6 million —and agreed to carry out the hit, first casing St. Peter's Square, then planning a small diversionary explosion to let Ağca do his job and escape.

Bad luck for him: there'd been no bomb, and he'd nearly been lynched by assembled worshipers after he'd wounded the pope and three bystanders. Some said it was a miracle that Ağca had survived, but the shooter might not think so. Italy had abolished capital punishment in 1948, but life in prison wouldn't be a picnic for a guy who'd tried to kill the pope. If Ağca lived through that and ever got parole, Turkey stood by extradite and try him for Abdi İpekçi's slaying, where mandatory death by hanging was imposed for twenty-nine different crimes including murder.

Meanwhile, Zilo Vassilev had been recalled to Sofia, skating on diplomatic immunity, while Bulgaria's National Police Service, embarrassed worldwide, finally had Bekir Çelenk locked up, spilling everything he knew about the Grey Wolves, pending extradition back to Turkey.

With all that going on, you might've thought the CIA would be forgotten for a while—but no such luck. *Los Angeles Times* reporter Robert Scheer had obtained former destroyer Captain John Herrick's 1964 log from the USS *Maddox*, declaring that the alleged North Vietnamese "ambush" of American ships in the Gulf of Tonkin never happened. The lie had been an open secret in clandestine circles for twenty-seven years, but now every literate person on Earth knew the Vietnam War's precipitating incident—LBJ's excuse for all that followed—was a total hoax.

Tough luck for somebody, Gantt thought. *Let Congress chase the Navy now, and hopefully forget the CIA even exists.*

———

LITTLE ITALY, Manhattan: May 28, 1981

"YOU EVER FEEL LIKE GETTING' outa here," Angelo Giordano asked, "and maybe headin' down to Florida? I mean, like movin' out for good?"

"I think a lotta things," Dominic answered him. "But I ain't runnin'. We was born here, right?"

"Don't mean we gotta die here, though,"

"We ain't dead yet."

"Not *yet,*" Ange said, changing the emphasis.

He had a point, Dom knew, but only *to* a point. Florida was the hot spot for cocaine, and Dom's family got its share from Medellín, mostly coming from Panama or the Bahamas, but while *La Commissione* had always viewed Miami as an "open city," meaning any family could do its share of business, there was more to worry about in Florida than stepping on the Trafficante Family's toes. Since last year's Mariel boatlift, the Sunshine State was rife with Cubans and Colombians, Bolivians and Puerto Ricans, plus so-called Jamaican "posses" known for dreadlocks and drive-by killings with Russian machine guns. Add to that some cops as dirty as the dealers, counting on their badges as a license to steal and resell captured drugs, and Miami was a three-ring circus out of Hell.

Not that Gotham and environs were much better, mind you.

Philip Testa's appointment as successor to Angelo Bruna hadn't settled anything in war-torn Philadelphia. In fact, the Ides of March had seen "Chicken Man" Testa killed by a nail bomb at his home, touching off another round of killings in Philly. Cops suspected underboss Peter Casella, working with *capo* Frank Narducci, but now *consigliere* Nicky Scarfo was blocking Casella's promotion, ensuring another gang war. Between attempts to kill each other, someone from the Casella or Scarfo factions had found time yesterday to take out Chelsais Bouras, leader of Philly's so-called Greek Mob.

Despite all that, Dom Giordano worried more about the bloodshed closer to home. The feds had locked up Bonanno Family boss Philip Rastelli two years ago, but he still ran his outfit from prison at Lewisburg, most recently suspecting treason from three of his *capos*: Dominick Trinchera, Philip Giaccone, and Alphonse "Sonny Red" Indelicato. On May 5th loyal *capos* Joe Massino and Dominick "Sonny Black" Napolitano invited the turncoats to a Brooklyn sit-down, where they were ambushed and shot by a hit team including three *mafiosi* on loan from Canada, then dismembered and buried at a vacant lot in Queens.

Who would be next?

Dom Giordano didn't know, but he was keeping his guard up and not accepting any social invitations for the next few months, at least. As he had learned from child-hood, at his father's knee, supposed friends often turned out to be the worst of enemies.

FBI FIELD OFFICE, Manhattan: July 8, 1981

ERIN O'HARA WATCHED her fellow special agent, Stephen Barnes, paging through memos on his desk, and frowned. Something about Barnes had been nagging at her almost from the day they'd met, and while she couldn't put her finger on it yet, she'd seen something in June that made her wonder...

Erin had come in late, wanting to catch up on paperwork she'd left unfinished from the afternoon and feeling guilty, even though she guessed she'd be the only day shift agent working overtime. But she'd been wrong. Barnes had been there, going through a batch of files she'd double-checked since then, containing leads on various suspected Soviet illegals operating both in New York City and in Washington, D.C.

So what? That was his job, the same as it was hers, but something in his manner, and the smile he'd seemed to force after he saw her watching him. Had she imagined just the slightest bit of guilt behind it?

Never mind.

Aside from tracking Reds the Bureau hadn't yet identified beyond their ever-changing codenames, Erin was still following the aftermath of Operation ABSCAM. Jurors had convicted Senator Harrison Williams in May, despite his claims that he'd been "selectively prosecuted" for backing Ted Kennedy's challenge to incumbent Jimmy Carter in last year's Democratic primaries. At least that farcical excuse made more sense than the senator's contention that he wasn't *really* bribed at all, because the

Bureau's phony Arab sheik had given him stock in a nonexistent titanium mine. He faced three years in prison if his long-winded appeals fell through, and the Senate had belatedly censured Williams rather than expelling him outright.

In July the House Ethics Committee had debated filing charges against John Murtha, splitting along party lines with the Republican majority deciding not to punish him. The committee's Democratic special counsel resigned in protest and Attorney General William Smith —formerly President Reagan's personal lawyer—ruled out prosecution on grounds that Murtha's "actual intent" was to obtain investment in his Pennsylvania district. Murtha finally "cleared his name" by testifying against fellow congressmen John Murphy of New York and Frank Thompson from New Jersey—both of whom the Bureau had on video accepting bribes and stuffing cash into their pockets.

Meanwhile, the House Subcommittee on Civil and Constitutional Rights continued its probe of FBI sting operations, predicted to last for another three years, but outgoing Attorney General Benjamin Civiletti had beat them to the punch in January, establishing new investigative guidelines requiring that regional SAC's "immediately" notify Bureau headquarters and the Assistant Attorney General in charge of the Criminal Division before they authorized any "extraordinary" moves regarding "serious" crimes. Erin knew that wouldn't satisfy the Bureau's critics—nothing ever did—but she thought it was fair enough.

And in the future, feeling slightly foolish even as she thought it, her attempts to ferret out Red spies would make room for covert surveillance of her fellow agent,

Stephen Barnes. If he was innocent, it wouldn't hurt him. If he wasn't...well, then that could be a feather in her cap, along with helping reinforce America's security.

————

SALT LAKE CITY, Utah: October 9, 1981

FOURTEEN MONTHS after his last attack, the still-unidentified UNABOM suspect had surfaced, putting Special Agent Wyman Gantt back on the road again—or, rather, in the air.

This time a janitor had found the bomb in a University of Utah business classroom and called campus security, who in turn had alerted the local bomb squad. It was defused without exploding, the components all intact, closely resembling hand-crafted parts of the serial bomber's previous parcels.

Now, the Bureau and Salt Lake City PD were scouring U of U's files, seeking anyone who might've nursed a grudge against the school for any reason. Past and present personnel were being scrutinized for gripes about dismissal, poor performance reviews, and failure to achieve promotion or tenure. Student suspects would include all those suspended or expelled, dropouts, those who'd complained of poor or failing grades, and those who had filed claims against the school for any reason, ranging from reports of bullying on campus to unprosecuted sexual assaults.

In short, it could be damned near anyone, not even looking at crackpot polygamists who held a grudge against state government in general.

There was no good news on the case so far, but some had come from Washington in April, when Justice went public with President Reagan's pardon of convicted former Bureau leaders Mark Felt and Edward Miller. Attorney General Edwin Meese had requested that action, and Reagan had complied in late March, though news of the pardons didn't break until April 15th, income tax filing day.

Reagan's pardon claimed the pair had served the Bureau and America "with great distinction," their convictions resulting from "good-faith belief" that their crimes were justified. "The record," Reagan or some flunky wrote, as if he'd actually seen their files, "demonstrates that they acted not with criminal intent, but in the belief that they had grants of authority reaching to the highest levels of government."

That's true enough, Gantt thought. At least three presidents and twice that number of attorneys general had known of and approved the COINTELPRO crimes without a word of protest between 1964 and Richard Nixon's resignation in disgrace.

Speaking of Tricky Dick, he'd sent Felt and Miller bottles of champagne when the pardon came through, each bearing a note that read "Justice ultimately prevailed." Nixon could say that, since his own pardon from Gerald Ford ensured that he would never spend a day in jail for all the shit he'd pulled as president. At a press conference following the announcement, Miller grinned and told the world, "I certainly owe the Gipper one."

Gantt wondered if such mercy would have saved his father, had the old man lived to be indicted with his nominal superiors now off the hook for good. And would it wait for *him,* if his own acts against the New Left finally caught up with him, somewhere down range?

Best not to think about that, he decided, and went back to studying schematics of the Unabomber's latest deadly toy.

———

ONE POLICE PLAZA, Manhattan: November 6, 1981

SERGEANT PAYTON SAWYER reckoned he was just about fed up with living in the past, yet it kept sneaking up on him and slapping him across the face.

Black Muslims, for example. Warith Deen Mohammed had officially dissolved his father's movement three years ago, but now Louis Farrakhan had revived the Nation of Islam, based in Chicago, publishing a new weekly paper titled *The Final Call* and vowing to reopen 130 defunct mosques nationwide. He wasn't making any special waves so far, but Sawyer wondered how long it would take for the patented blasts against Jews and police to resume.

He tabled that problem for now, and focused on a more immediate concern, namely the Black Liberation Army's apparent revival. Described as dead or dying more than twelve months back, the BLA was obviously still alive and kicking—unlike three more officers its members had gunned down.

NYPD Patrolman John Scarangella was the year's first fatality. With partner Richard Rainey, he'd stopped a van in Queens, noting the ride's resemblance to a vehicle reported near the scene of several recent burglaries. Unknown to the patrolmen, the van's occupants were ex-Black Panthers and BLA members Anthony LaBorde and James York, now known as "Abdul Majid" and "Bashir Hameed," respectively. They'd jumped out firing thirty pistol shots, striking Scarangella twice in the head, wounding Rainey fourteen times. Scarangella had died two weeks later, while Rainey left the department on a disability pension. Both gunmen were at large, facing twenty-five years to life if convicted at trial.

What happened next, if possible, was even worse.

Perusing the available reports, Sawyer knew that the militants involved were black *and* white, both male and female. Headquarters and people from the FBI assumed the whites were remnants of a Weather Underground spinoff group, the May 19 Communist Movement, merged with BLA survivors into a "Revolutionary Armed Task Force."

What it boiled down to was an armored truck robbery in Nanuet, twenty-seven miles north of Gotham, that left one Brink's guard dead and another wounded, paying the bandits $1.6 million. While the raiders fled through Nyack, five miles east of Nanuet on the Hudson River, police gave chase and a second firefight erupted, killing two officers and wounding another.

It sounded simple on paper, but out on the streets it was chaos.

The trouble started at Nanuet Mall, at 3:55 p.m. on October 20th, as Brink's guards Peter Paige and Joseph Trombino emerged with bags of cash from their daily pickup. Gunmen leaping from a van nearby cut loose with a shotgun and M16 rifle, killing Paige outright, nearly severing Trombino's arm after he'd fired a single round.

The Brink's driver returned fire from his armored cab but couldn't get a decent shot.

Seizing the loot, the robbers sped off to a meeting place where comrades waited with a yellow Honda and a rented U-Haul truck. While police units scrambled throughout Rockland County, a witness saw and reported the vehicle switch, describing the getaway rides. Soon, Nanuet officers Waverly Brown, Artie Keenan, Brian Lennon and Edward O'Grady spotted both vehicles, stopping them on an entrance ramp to the New York State Thruway off State Route 59. They saw white faces—confusing, since early reports said the bandits were black—but still approached with drawn pistols. At the U-Haul's wheel, Weatherman fugitive Kathy Boudin played dumb and fearful, prompting the cops to lower their guns, then cohorts wearing body armor came out firing automatic weapons, spraying the landscape.

Officer Brown fell first, wounded, then one of the shooters walked up and finished him off at close range. O'Grady emptied his revolver, then suffered fatal wounds while reloading. Keenan took a bullet to the leg and ducked behind a tree, returning fire. The U-Haul rammed Lennon's cruiser, trapping him between O'Grady's body and a crumpled door, still firing as the bandits scattered. Boudin fled on foot, others piling into the Honda, a couple of their cronies carjacking a dazed passerby.

The plan had gone to hell from there. An off-duty prison guard caught Boudin and held her, despite her claims that she was "Barbara Edson," an innocent bystander. Fugitives David Gilbert, Judith Clark and Samuel Brown crashed their Honda while making a sharp turn, injuring Brown's neck and causing Clark to drop her pistol just as South Nyack Police Chief Alan Colsey arrived and held them at gunpoint. The trio went to jail, while officers recovered Clark's gun and half of the Brink's loot.

From there, the plot began unraveling. Officers traced the Honda's license number to a New Jersey apartment rented by prison escapee Marilyn Buck, there seizing weapons, explosives, and detailed blueprints of six NYPD precinct houses in Manhattan. Papers found in Buck's flat led to another address in Mt. Vernon, Westchester County, where raiders found more guns and ammo, ski masks, and bloodied clothing from a wounded bandit. Running neighborhood license tags through the FBI's National Crime Information Center, officers identified one suspect vehicle as a 1978 Chrysler, spotted on October 23rd. The occupants tried to flee, then stopped to shoot it out. Police killed BLA veteran Samuel Smith, arresting compatriot Nathaniel Burns.

Still in the wind so far were Buck, plus BLA members Samuel Brown, Cecilio "Chui" Ferguson, Edward Joseph, Donald Weems, and Jeral Williams. Arrests were predicted "soon," but who could say for sure? Just yesterday, the BLA had released a communiqué claiming credit for the Brink's heist on behalf of the RATF, allegedly collaborating with "North American Anti-Imperialists" whose white members, the paper claimed, had infiltrated redneck racist groups to I.D. future targets for elimination.

Sawyer didn't mind a bit if black and white fanatics started killing one another, but he worried about cops caught in the middle, dying in the crossfire.

Especially if he were one of them.

———

MORAZÁN DEPARTMENT, El Salvador: December 12, 1981

OVERNIGHT, the village of El Mozote—roughly 110 miles east of San Salvador, near the Honduran border—had ceased to exist. Its population was annihilated, every building torched, in what the Atlacatl Battalion's field commander called "an example" to other FMLN rebels.

And Hardy Gantt, in his capacity as an observer for the CIA, had seen it all.

The massacre had been part of a sweep through Morazán Department, following identical campaigns in other provinces. Authorities in San Salvador called it "draining the sea"—a reference to Mao Zedong's comment that "The guerrilla must move amongst the people as a fish swims in the sea." To "drain" that human sea, the military bombed, strafed and shelled supposed rebel districts with a vengeance, often—as at El Mozote—sending ground troops in to slaughter residents of suspect villages.

The first sweep, back in March, had occurred in northern El Salvador's Cabañas Department, indiscriminately slaying hundreds, then pursuing some 4,000 refugees—mostly women and children—to the Rio Lempa, trapping them between the Atlacatl Battalion and Honduran troops on the other side. Warplanes arrived, bombing and strafing the unarmed survivors, killing hundreds more.

A second offensive ravaged Cabañas Department in November, picking up where the earlier slaughter left off, with U.S. advisors along for the show, describing the Atlacatl Battalion's random killers as "the pride of the United States military team in San Salvador," battling heroically to "turn a losing war around." Their tactics included beheading with a mobile guillotine and using a rural meat packing plant to dispose of remains.

The slaughter was no secret. In its spring report, Amnesty International named Salvadoran military and security units as "responsible for widespread torture, mutilation and killings of noncombatant civilians from all sectors of Salvadoran society." Socorro Jurídico, the Catholic Archdiocesan Legal Aid Society, had counted 13,353 summary executions so far this year, a number widely viewed as too conservative.

And now, they'd have to add in El Mozote.

Gantt wasn't sure how many men, women and kids the Atlacatl Battalion had murdered by gunfire or hanging. He'd stopped counting somewhere around 800, not surprised after the shit he'd seen in Southeast Asia, making no protest, simply observing what the state called "cleansing." He'd been sickened by the rapes, including those of minors, and the soldiers bragging of their preference for ten-to-twelve-year-olds, but Langley wouldn't thank him if he mentioned *that* deranged behavior in his field report.

Besides, he wasn't finished yet. While smoke still rose from burning homes, there was another village waiting to be "cleansed," a few miles farther down the road.

And Washington, of course, remained oblivious to what its influence, weapons and cash had wrought. It didn't matter that a former Uruguayan intelligence officer had revealed use of CIA torture manuals in his country, or that Argentina's "dirty war" still rolled along with U.S. backing. Curiously, Congress *had* cut off funding to Contra death squads in Nicaragua, but that didn't faze the Reagan White House. Spooks like Lieutenant-Colonel Oliver North had solicited $10 million from the Sultan of

Brunei, while peddling weapons to the same Iranian government that had only recently freed a pack of American hostages. And when all else failed, there was always cocaine in abundance, keeping up the time-honored tradition of Agency heroin smugglers from Europe in the late 1940s and from Vietnam during its twenty years of war.

The only rule was *Don't get caught,* and Gantt couldn't help wondering if some of his superiors were riding for a big-time fall.

———

CENTRAL PARK, Manhattan: December 14, 1981

"BEING WATCHED, YOU SAY?" Lieutenant-Colonel Alexander Bobrik of the KGB repeated back what Agent Stephen Barnes had said just seconds earlier, sounding more nonchalant than Barnes expected.

"*Maybe* being watched," Barnes said. "I can't prove anything so far."

"By this O'Hara woman?"

"Possibly." Barnes couldn't bring himself to say it might all be a figment of his overwrought imagination.

"But she has said nothing of this to your mutual superiors?"

"Nothing that I'm aware of," Barnes admitted.

"And you suspect this...why, again? Because the two of you were moonlighting?"

Barnes grimaced at the malaprop. "Not moonlighting," he said. "That means working a second job. The two of us were working *overtime*, not that unusual, and I glanced up to find here looking at me. Staring, really. Not that anything was said, at least to me."

"And she observed you doing something...illegitimate?"

"Nothing like that. Just looking over files I planned to photograph later, but I postponed that to be safe."

"If she suspected you of something, and she passed that on, would you be made aware of it?"

Barnes frowned at that, considering. "Not necessarily. They might put someone on me, trying not to make it obvious. Approaching me right off would make surveillance difficult, maybe impossible. They might have someone follow me around or tap my office phone, the way they did with Coplon years ago."

"That cost us much prestige and bad publicity," said Bobrik. Slowly swiveling his head, he added, "Are you certain no one followed you today?"

"I'm positive," Barnes said. "It took me twice as long to get here. Trust me."

"Very well, with the proviso that the consequences of a failure due to negligence would be...severe."

"I understand that."

"Then we shall proceed. Moscow requires more information on your government's response to our Afghan activities, particularly details of the so-called Reagan Doctrine."

"That's more CIA than FBI," Barnes said, certain that Bobrik knew as much already. "But I'll get you what I can, of course."

In simple terms, he knew the Reagan Doctrine was an all-out bid to undercut and overwhelm Soviet influence around the world, angling to end the Cold War if it all worked out as planned.

"And Solidarity," said Bobrik, almost as an afterthought.

Barnes knew about the Polish labor union founded fifteen months ago and led by Lech Wałęsa, prompting Wojciech Jaruzelski, First Secretary of the Polish Communist Party, to impose martial law as a hedge against Soviet intervention.

"The only thing we're getting about that, so far, is notice of celebrity fund-raisers. But sure, I'll copy what I can and pass it on."

"So be it. Until next time, then, and I need not remind you of the need for utmost caution."

"No, you don't," Barnes answered.

Thinking to himself, *But you just did.*

———

FBI HEADQUARTERS: December 23, 1981

TWO DAYS UNTIL CHRISTMAS, and the Bureau wasn't letting up on radicals over the holidays. A good thing, too, in Agent Devon Gantt's opinion, since subversives cared no more for celebration of religious holidays than for the price of tea in China—whatever the hell that was.

Black militants were still at large across the land, not only robbing armored cars but building communes, killing cops who tried to rein them in. Take Philadelphia, the first U.S. capital city. "John Africa's" MOVE cult had pulled up stakes and found new digs in West Philly's Cobb Creek district, starting a new open-air trash dump and blasting their "gospel" from loudspeakers 24/7. One alleged black journalist who'd covered them extensively—

former Black Panther Wesley Cook, aka "Mumia Abu-Jamal"—was facing murder charges now, after he'd shot and killed Patrolman Daniel Faulker. Cook claimed that he'd been driving night shifts in a taxi and coincidentally discovered Faulker beating up Mumia's younger brother, jumping in to stop it. In the struggle, Wesley took a bullet to the stomach but survived it. Faulkner didn't. He had four slugs in his back, one in his face, delivered as a *coup de grâce*. Responding officers found Wesley at the scene, gun still clutched in his hand.

More leftist cop-killers at large were operating as the UFF—"United Freedom Front"—founded in 1975 as the "Sam Melville/Jonathan Jackson Unit" by two Vietnam vets who'd met in prison. Though taking their outfit's first name from two dead black radicals, the group's founders and members were lily-white, fond of robbing banks and bombing targets that included South African Airways, Union Carbide, IBM, Mobil Oil, military bases and courthouses. Since yesterday, they were prime suspects in the murder of New Jersey State Trooper Philip Lamonaco, shot in Warren County, near the Pennsylvania border. Investigators found the killers' shot-up car nearby, and they were fanning out from there, with no arrests in sight.

Another nonsurprise: while news of government atrocities kept coming from El Salvador, U.S. support for Red guerillas was increasing, mostly generated by CISPES. The Bureau had been looking into it, seeking potential violations of the Foreign Agents Registration Act, and while they'd found nothing, some liberal reporters got the scent and started running articles about the "bad old days" of COINTELPRO coming back. Director Webster, through his press flacks, tried to claim the Bureau was "inquiring," rather than "investigating," as if that made any difference. Devon liked Webster well enough, but on this point he'd sounded mealy-mouthed.

Gantt understood that praising Edgar Hoover was a no-no, since the Old Man's crimes had been so thoroughly exposed, but still he had to wonder, what was happening to the United States?

CHAPTER 9

UNIVERSITY OF CALIFORNIA, BERKELEY: JULY 4, 1982

FEW STUDENTS WERE around campus on Independence Day, which made it nice for Special Agent Wyman Gantt. The few he saw were likely bound for lunch, since campus libraries and offices were closed and the first six-week summer session was behind them, the second beginning on Tuesday.

It struck Gantt as an odd time for the Unabomber to touch off another campus blast, but maybe he (or she) was more concerned with sending messages than racking up a body count.

The year's first bomb—indeed, the first in seven months—had detonated in Nashville, at Vanderbilt University, back on May 5th. It came by mail as usual, addressed to the head of the school's computer department, but wounded his secretary instead, leaving her with shrapnel wounds and major burns.

At Berkeley, two days earlier, there'd been a twist.

Instead of mailing the device, it was disguised inside a can, left in a common room of the computer science wing on Friday, injuring a random professor who'd picked it up.

Both victims would survive, but Wyman wouldn't bet on them forgetting. Back at headquarters, the UNABOM task force was getting nowhere fast.

He'd been relieved when a federal court restored ex-Associate Director Mark Felt's law license, based on President Reagan's pardon from a felony conviction. Felt and fellow clemency recipient Ed Miller had appeared before the Senate's Subcommmittee on Terrorism in June, both ardently declaring that Attorney General Edward Levi's guidelines for Bureau investigations were putting the country at risk.

Gantt saw their point, and wouldn't disagree if he were asked, but even while he'd been an undercover "Beard" assigned to the New Left, doing whatever was required to make cases, whether they went to trial or not, a question had bedeviled him. What did it say about a so-called democratic nation when its law enforcement offices could only keep uneasy peace by breaking laws themselves?

Wyman still had no answer, but he knew one thing: if he could just have thirty seconds with the Unabomber, on his own, he'd put the bastard down and never lose a minute's sleep about it afterward.

———

San Vincente Department, El Salvador: August 22, 1982

CIA FIELD AGENT Hardy Gantt breathed in the stench of blood and gunsmoke, thinking to himself, *Another day, another massacre, bankrolled from Washington under the guise of "national security."*

He understood the thought process at Langley and approved of it, up to a point. Increasingly, however, he'd begun to wonder if the Agency had done more harm than good so far in Latin America—or where he'd been assigned before this tour, in Southeast Asia.

At least El Calabozo—"The Dungeon," in English—wasn't a village, which spared Gantt from standing around with a thumb up his ass while the American-trained Atlacatl Battalion completed its task of mass murder. Government troops had made another of their sweeps through the province, twenty-odd miles east of San Salvador, torching "hostile" villages and driving displaced occupants before them till they reached the Amatitán River and could go no farther without boats. Surrounded, 217 alleged FMLN supporters—none armed, many of them children—made easy targets for the concentrated fire of rifles and machine guns purchased mostly from the States.

Minister of Defense José Guillermo García was still denying the occurrence of December's massacre at El Mozote when the new atrocity went down, No one with any sense believed him, but it didn't matter, with the Reagan White House solidly behind President Álvaro Magaña, leader of the so-called Christian Democratic Party that had stepped up to replace the former Revolutionary Junta without any change that Gantt could see in its despotic style.

The FMLN claimed it wanted to set up a "government of broad participation," which President Reagan labeled communism. He'd preferred Magaña's predecessor, far-right National Republican Alliance leader and death squad commando Roberto D'Aubuisson, but would settle for Magaña—until May, the president of El Salvador's largest mortgage bank. Reagan loved banks in general, as demonstrated by his drive to deregulate America's savings and loan indstry, gleefully telling his cronies, "I think we just hit the jackpot!"

Now, watching soldiers roll their victims into the river, some corpses doused with acid beforehand, Gantt reflected—not for the first time—that most Americans would probably be outraged if they saw first-hand what their tax dollars were supporting. As it was, though, few among them seemed to give a damn, preferring to watch *Cheers* and *Newhart* on TV, or laugh along with *M*A*S*H* as it turned the Korean War into a comedy routine.

Wherever Hardy looked these days, it was the same. In Honduras, Washington-supported Intelligence Battalion 3-16 had started calling itself the Special Intelligence Branch under General Gustavo Álvarez, but its members still used the CIA's *Counterintelligence Interrogation* manual for tips on torturing political prisoners.

Congress had banned support for Nicaraguan death squads last year, when they were caught raping and murdering American nuns, but that hadn't stopped the Agency from meeting with Contra leaders in Costa Rica. That meeting's purpose, in the words of an inside report from the CIA's Directorate of Operations: "an exchange in the United States of narcotics for arms, which then are shipped to Nicaragua." Beyond that, when DEA agents in San Francisco seized $36,800 from Edward Meneses, Langley's pet drug runner, the Agency's Inspector General demanded return of the money "to protect an operational equity, i.e., a Contra support group in which it had an operational interest."

None or that surprised Hardy. His late father Aloysius, an OSS/CIA pioneer, had been forthright in explaining how the Agency did business before Hardy made his choice to join. In general, he still believed ends justified the means...but then he looked at lifeless children and their mothers, their grandparents, floating down the river, and he had to wonder if at least a portion of his soul was out there with them, sinking fast.

———

BEIRUT, Lebanon: September 22, 1982

ONE YEAR away from mandatory retirement, and Colby Gantt couldn't believe he'd drawn another field assignment at his age—and to Lebanon, yet, where full-scale civil war had been raging for seven years now, with no end in sight.

At times, you couldn't tell the Lebanese players without a program. The war had begun as sectarian violence between so-called Christian militias and a left-wing alliance including Yasser Arafat's Palestine Liberation Organization, plus Druze and Muslim guerillas. In June 1976 President Elias Sarkis ordered government troops to "restore peace" by backing the Christians. Four months later, that idea had failed so monumentally that the Arab League—which founded the PLO back in 1964—created its own predominantly Syrian Arab Deterrent Force to stand between the murderous belligerents. On top of that, tribal drug lords ruled the Beqaa Valley, as had their ancestors before them, dating back to the Roman Empire.

Matters had gone from bad to worse in June—if that were even possible—when PLO members launched attacks on Israel from Lebanon, prompting Tel Aviv's third invasion since 1978. With worthless guarantees of peace to come, Israelis lifted their siege of Beirut, then returned in mid-September, three weeks after right-wing Christian Phalange Party leader Bachir Gemayel's election as Lebanon's president, when bombers killed Gemayel and twenty-six followers at party headquarters. Top that off with the Sabra and Shatila massacres two days later, killing 3,500 Palestinian and Lebanese Shiite civilians, and you got the picture.

Beirut was a suppurating slice of Hell on Earth. Even shut up in the U.S. embassy downtown, Colby could hear the gunfire and explosions. Despite its air-conditioning, the smell of death was unavoidable.

If Langley's masters had to send him somewhere for his last hurrah, why couldn't it have been to London, where Vatican moneyman Roberto Calvi, aka "God's Banker," had been found in June, hanging beneath Blackfriars Bridge after traveling from Rome via Zurich on a false passport? Italian police had their eyes on Sicilian *mafioso* Giuseppe Calò and another suspect, Sardinian businessman Flavio Carboni, whose "wide-ranging interests" included high-level fraud and collusion with the sinister P2 Masonic lodge in all manner of covert activity.

For that matter, Langley could have shipped Gantt off to Rome, sniffing around the scandal-ridden Banco Ambrosiano's reputed diversion of Vatican funds into narcotics smuggling and terrorism. While there, Colby could have detoured to Florence, offering advice on the so far fruitless pursuit of a serial killer who murdered couples on rural lovers' lanes, shooting the men and mailing pieces of their girlfriends to police headquarters.

Almost *anywhere* on Earth, in fact, was better than stinking Beirut.

But it was out of his hands now, leaving him stuck with the words of Alfred Lord Tennyson's "Charge of the Light Brigade."

Ours not to wonder why, ours but to do or die.

And wasn't that some happy shit?

———

FONTAINEBLEAU HOTEL, *Miami Beach: October 25, 1982*

LOUNGING AT POOLSIDE, sleekly oiled and barely dressed in skimpy Speedo swim trunks from Australia, Dominic Giordano thought he just might love working vacations. There'd been time to play, of course, and would again before he flew back to New York, but for the moment, all he had to do was catch some rays and watch the babes around him, wearing little more than he was.

Florida could grow on him, Dom thought, especially when winter froze Gotham in snow and ice.

Speaking of snow, he'd cut another deal last night with Jorge Ochoa, traveling salesman for the Medellín Cartel, that would increase the Giordano Family's monthly cocaine shipment at a price of $60,000 per kilo on delivery. Once that was cut and parceled out in grams, the family's return would be around $125,000, minus what Gotham's cops required to keep the traffic flowing without interruption. Call it a 150-percent markup, and Dom was glad to take that all day long.

Of course, the goddamned feds were horning in as usual. In January, Attorney General William Smith had shuffled things around in Washington, so that the DEA's director was reporting to the top man of the FBI, sharing jurisdiction over the Controlled Substances Act of 1971. Neither alpha dog played well with others, which was fine with Dom, as long as he had cover from NYPD. In his mind, last week's creation of an Organized Crime Drug Enforcement Task Force, combining elements of eleven different federal agencies, only confused matters more for the so-called "good guys."

On Dom's end, he worried more about getting whacked than getting busted. It had taken seven years for lawmen to admit what he'd known all along—that Jimmy Hoffa was dead and gone for good—and now people kept dying in Gotham. The latest, smooth-talking husband-wife con artists Michael and Nicolina Lizak were technically missing persons who'd vanished back in March, while driving from Staten Island to Atlantic City for an "extended vacation." Cops found their car abandoned in Brooklyn, an odd coincidence, considering that Nicolena's brother-in-law, Robert Russo, had been murdered at his Staten Island home last November.

Detectives weren't "positively connecting" the two incidents, but then again, they likely didn't share Dom Giordano's knowledge of the story's background. Bobby Russo was—*had been*—a soldier with the Gambino Family, whose current boss, Paul Castellano, had the Lizak's pegged as Russo's killers. To Dom, their disappearance was a simple case of *quid pro quo* payback, and if anybody ever found the missing couple, they'd be hard pressed to identify the stiffs.

Business as usual, Dom thought, sipping his second Mai Tai of the day and ruminating, *Better them than me.*

———

BIRMINGHAM, *Alabama: November 3, 1982*

THE DEMOCRATIC PRIMARY results were in, and Dave Jordan wasn't surprised by the result. George Wallace, as expected, had won a fourth term as governor, but this time he appeared to be a very different man.

So far, at least. Jordan supposed he'd have to wait and see.

Three years ago, Wallace told Alabamians that he'd been "born again." Of course, he'd claimed to be a Christian all along, but this presumably was something stronger, more significant. At the same time, regarding his long fight for segregation, Wallace told reporters, "I was wrong. Those days are over, and they ought to be over." He'd asked blacks to forgive him, while Klan leaders wailed that their old hero "wasn't white anymore."

It hadn't hurt during September's Democratic primaries, when Wallace led a field of five potential candidates with 43 percent. Two weeks later, in a runoff against Lieutenant Governor George McMillan,Wallace had claimed the narrowest win of his life, 51 percent to 49. Today, he'd pulled it out, beating Montgomery's Republican mayor and five fringe candidates with 58 percent of the popular vote.

But would Wallace keep his word? Or was his turnaround simply a ploy, ducking some of the condemnation he'd received for the unabashed bigotry of his last campaign, when the "old" George had reaped 83 percent of the state's ballots?

"I still don't like him," Fee O'Hara said, as she leaned forward to refill her glass of chardonnay.

"No second chances for a change of heart?" Dave asked.

She flicked a glance at him, frowning, and answered, "Only if I trust someone. They have to earn it first." And then: "You getting tired, or what?"

They hadn't been to bed in nearly two weeks, but now David saw a chance, however slim. "I'm getting there," he said.

———

HARLEM: November 15, 1982

LOOKING AROUND HIS SAD APARTMENT, NYPD Sergeant Payton Sawyer realized he'd occupied the same small, sparsely decorated place for almost twenty years. It suited him all right, but now he wondered if the flat might be symbolic of his job—even his life—frozen in time and stagnating.

He couldn't say that of the outside world.

Chicago, for example. In the case arising from the state's killing of three Black Panthers thirteen years ago, the feds had settled for $1.85 million, split between the mothers of Fred Hampton and Mark Clark. Their lawyer told reporters that the settlement was a confession of conspiracy between the FBI and local cops; the opposition's lawyers stolidly denied it, trying to convince their listeners that paying up wasn't admitting guilt.

Sawyer knew that was a crock of shit, and wondered if he should've joined the lawsuit after all. Those cops had killed his brother, right along with Clark and Hampton, meaning that the settlement would likely have been larger. Payton reckoned he could use $600,000 toward retirement, coming up before much longer, but he had preferred to keep his head down, draw no flack at work, and let it go. The way he saw it, when his brother quit the FBI and wound up in the Panthers, of all things, it almost counted as a kind of suicide.

Meanwhile, the roundup of October's homicidal Brink's bandits from Nanuet and Nyack was proceeding, more or less. Charges had been filed against the raiders now in custody, and fugitive Jeral Williams had been added to the FBI's "Most Wanted" list on July 23rd, still dodging manhunters. Eight weeks later, a Manhattan judge had called off pretrial hearings due to raving court-room outbursts from defendants Sam Brown, Nathaniel Burns, Kathy Boudin, Judith Clark, David Gilbert, Anthony LaBorde and Donald Weems. They'd shouted, "Free the land!" while being led away in chains, but Payton saw no freedom in their futures.

Now had come official word of more arrests, those captured in the past couple of days including BLA members William Johnson, Edward Joseph and James York, with ex-Weathermen Silvia Baraldini and Marilyn Buck. Baraldini's charges also included JoAnne Chesimard's prison break. Still in the wind with Jeral Williams were Cynthia Boston and Cheri Dalton, all allegedly defectors from the dying BLA to the Republic of New Afrika.

Payton didn't know whether the feds would ever bag them all, and now he was surprised to find he hardly cared. Whatever happened next, whatever shit they tried to pull, he knew that they were running out of time.

Like everyone, he thought, *including me.* Scowling, he went to fetch a beer.

————

FBI Headquarters: December 17, 1982

JUST WHEN AGENT DEVON GANTT thought trouble had begun to fade on the New Left, it started up again. There'd been no change so far under the Reagan White House team, for all their tough talk—or, at least, no change for the better.

One thing gratifying to the Bureau was the trial of Wesley Cook, aka "Mumia Abu-Jamal," for cop-killing in Philadelphia. Gantt had taken time to look up Cook's street name, discovering that "Mumia" supposedly meant "Prince" in Swahili, while "Abu-Jamal" translated as "father of Jamal"—a reference to Cook's son from his failed first marriage.

Whatever. The good news was that Judge Albert Sabo had warned Cook about disruptive outbursts at his trial, denying his right to self-defense and forcing him to accept an underfunded lawyer playing catchup on the case. Three crime scene witnesses described Cook shooting Officer Daniel Faulkner, while two more—a cop and a nurse—swore he'd confessed from his hospital bed, saying, "I shot the motherfucker and I hope the motherfucker dies." That was all jurors needed to hear, voting to convict him and imposing a death sentence.

The bad news: although Pennsylvania had restored

capital punishment six years ago, it hadn't executed anybody yet, and Cook might well keep on filing appeals until the next millennium.

On the white radical front, G-men and local police were still hunting members of the United Freedom Front, formerly the Sam Melville/Jonathan Jackson Unit, founded by Raymond Luc Levasseur, Tom Manning, and their wives back in 1975. One of their converts—Christopher King—aka "Kazi Toure," translated from Swahili as "hard work"—had been jailed in Massachusetts after State Troopers Michael Crosby and Paul Landry were shot in February, at a highway rest stop in North Attleborough. Both officers survived, and while they blamed the shooting on UFF member Jaan Laaman, a native Estonian who'd escaped in the confusion, King was carrying a gun and thus was named as an accomplice to attempted murder. Instead, jurors convicted him on firearms possession charges and sent him away. Laaman was still at large, sought in connection with various bombings spanning six years, plus last December's murder of New Jersey State Trooper Philip Lamonaco.

Never resting, the UFF had set off two bombs yesterday, damaging the South African Airlines office in Queens, New York, and an IBM office in Harrison, twenty-five miles farther north. Gantt wished the rats would blow themselves to smithereens, like the Greenwich Village Weathermen in 1970, but he supposed that was too much to hope for.

As long as they were captured, preferably killed while resisting arrest, it was all the same to him.

———

FBI FIELD OFFICE, Manhattan: December 17, 1982

THE MORE ERIN O'HARA saw of fellow agent Stephen Barnes, the less she felt at ease with him. She'd tried to tell herself that it was all imagination, she had nothing on him and she likely never would, but still...

She couldn't shake the sense that there was something *off* about him, something hinky, even if she didn't have a single piece of evidence to nail it down.

They'd worked together well enough so far, sharing opinions on the rumors gleaned from various informers, hinting at a Russian spy at large in Gotham, but the flimsy leads had taken them nowhere. If asked by one of her superiors, she'd have to say that Barnes seemed to be working diligently, running down the gossip they'd received, and Erin couldn't blame him if it went nowhere.

If only he would make a slip somehow, do something —*any*thing—to rate examination by the Bureau's Office of Professional Responsibility, she could accept the ruling handed down and let it go. But the suspense, made-up or otherwise, kept nagging at her day and night.

Whenever possible, Erin distracted herself by keeping track of Operation ABSCAM. Florida Congressman Richard Kelly claimed he was only "pretending" to accept $25,000 in Bureau bribes, secretly conducting his own private investigation and spending most of the money to support his "cover," but jurors still convicted him, resulting in an eighteen-month sentence. On appeal, his conviction was reversed on grounds of entrapment, but then a higher court affirmed the sentence and he'd finally gone off to prison.

Meanwhile, in March, senators debated expulsion of

colleague Harrison Williams but opted for censure instead, lately establishing a Select Committee to Study Undercover Activities that claimed sting operations "create serious risks to citizens' property, privacy, and civil liberties, and may compromise law enforcement itself." Media editorials and letters written to Bureau headquarters seemed to agree for the most part, making Erin wonder if new laws would be enacted to define what special agents could and couldn't do in the pursuit of criminals.

When pondering that began to make her head ache, Erin willed herself to let it go...and turned her mind back to the maybe-mystery of Agent Barnes.

————

FBI FIELD OFFICE, Manhattan: December 18, 1982

SEEING Erin O'Hara at her desk, Stephen Barnes wished he were a mind-reader. He hadn't actually caught her watching him per se, much less trailing him outside the office, but his instinct told Barnes there was something out of whack about her.

Knowing that he didn't dare confront O'Hara openly, he'd already begun to think of other options for side-tracking any doubts that she might have about him. And if worse came to worst, he might have to remove her entirely.

Enforcing federal laws, as Barnes well knew, could be a hazardous profession.

In the meantime, he was tracking turmoil in the Russian capital that might affect him, somewhere down the line. In January a stroke had killed Mikhail Suslov, a hardline Stalinist ensconced as Second Secretary of the Communist Party and its unofficial chief ideologue since 1965. Just days before his death, KGB Chairman Yuri Andropov had revealed to Suslov that Deputy KGB Chairman Semyon Tsvigun had shielded Andropov's children from corruption charges. Self-righteous Suslov was hounding Tsvigun to confess his crimes when Tsvigun died on January 19th, allegedly from diabetes, then Suslov dropped dead six days later, before he could plot his next move.

As for Andropov, he'd resigned from his KGB post on May 26th, promoted the same day to fill Suslov's empty position. Mere fortuitous coincidence?

Andropov's replacement as KGB Chairman was Vitaly Fedorchuk, previously head of the Ukraininan KGB since 1970, renowned for harsh suppression of that sector's militant nationalists. Alas, his tenure at Dzerzhinsky Square was brief, ending yesterday with his promotion to serve as Russia's Minister of Internal Affairs. His successor, former KGB Assistant Director Viktor Chebrikov, now pressed the same corruption probe that forced his boss, Andropov, to cover his children's financial tracks.

Andropov, all the while, continued to lead a charmed life. General Secretary Leonid Brezhnev had survived a major stroke in May, refusing to step down although he'd minimized public appearances. When surfaced on November 7th, in bitter cold for the annual celebration of Lenin's revolution, it proved too much, and a heart attack finally killed him three days later. His successor to the throne: Yuri Andropov.

All of that occurred against the backdrop of Afghanistan, where CIA support for mujahideen guerrillas had turned Russia's incursion into a proxy war on par with Spain's in the 1930s. None of the belligerents would yield, and as atrocities abounded, so did saber-rattling from Washington and Moscow.

Shrugging off the things he couldn't change, Barnes focused on his lifelong goal, his *father's* goal, of wreaking havoc from within the hated FBI. He would let no one stop him now, not from headquarters at the Hoover Building in D.C., or in his own backyard.

At any cost, he would proceed.

CHAPTER 10

BEIRUT: APRIL 18,1983

NOBODY in the U.S. Embassy downtown felt safe these days. The civil war—a three- or four-way battle for control —had only gotten worse over the past eight months, since the Multinational Force in Lebanon was created, including 800 members of the 32nd U.S. Marine Amphibious Unit, 800 Italian soldiers, and 400 French troops. Net results in "peacekeeping": zero, as far as Colby Gantt could tell.

President Reagan had recalled the 32nd MAU on September 10th, then—ever indecisive—sent them back on the 29th, by which time the MNF had grown to 2,200 French and Italian troops. Marines of the 24th MAU relieved the 32nd on October 30th, then the 32nd had returned again, renamed the 22nd for some reason fathomable only to the Pentagon. There matters stood today, with peace, the hopeless dream, no more in evidence that since the Israeli invasion tried and failed to put things right.

The native Lebanese, regardless of which side they'd chosen in the conflict, universally resented the Multinational Force. Muslims, particularly Shiites dwelling in the slums of West Beirut, believed the MNF favored their Maronite Christian opponents. As a result, most of their fire was aimed at foreigners in uniform and their respective embassies. Gantt, after three requests to Langley, had received permission to get out. The questions preying on him now were *how* and *when*.

The run to Beirut International Airport was perilous, even in armored vehicles, but Colby was prepared to take that chance, if he could ever get a ride. Ambassador Robert "Call Me Bob" Dillon was hard to pin down, and military convoys didn't roll unless he consulted with the 22nd MAU's commanding officer—which hadn't happened yet, in Colby's case. Now it was coming up on 3:00 p.m., another day nearly gone by, and Gantt was in a mood to corner the ambassador, reminding him in no uncertain terms that Langley had requested his return stateside without further delay.

Leaving his tiny office, Gantt immediately saw that something was amiss. People were scurrying about, jabbering back and forth excitedly, and there went Bob Dillon, rushing along the corridor with his personal secretary trying to keep up.

Gantt buttonholed a young guy from the passport office, stopped him in his tracks, asking him, "What's the problem?"

Blinking back at him, the youngster stammered out, "Some kind of panel truck... delivery...broke through somehow and hit the—"

That was all the kid got out before a massive blast ripped through the building, spraying shards of glass and chunks of masonry like automatic gunfire. Something struck Gantt's head with force enough to knock him down, and as he fell, he had the damnedest feeling that the floor was opening beneath him, pitching him head-long into the smoking maw of Hell.

———

FBI Headquarters: April 23, 1983

Colby was coming home today and Devon Gantt—his twin, eight minutes younger—was supposed to meet him when his flight touched down at Dulles International Airport in one hour and thirteen minutes. Devon had been granted time off for the rendezvous but had declined, showed up for work this Monday morning as he always had before, if not precisely in his usual condition.

And so what if he'd downed two stiff shots of Dewar's whisky in the place of breakfast? If somebody smelled it on his breath and took offense—hell, if they took it in their heads to fire his ass six months before retirement—who gave a damn?

Not Devon, and not Colby, either. Colby wouldn't smell him, wouldn't even *see* him, tucked inside his coffin, riding in the McDonnell Douglas C-9's cargo hold with sixteen other lifeless victims from the Beirut embassy bombing.

Devon had been over reports about the blast until his eyes and brain could take no more of it. He knew exactly how the suicide bomber had steered his van—first sold in

Texas, later purchased used and shipped out to the Middle East—beneath the embassy's horseshoe-shaped portico, then flipped a switch to set off a ton of explosives, probably squealing, "*Allāhu akbar!*"

The blast had collapsed the building's façade, dropping balconies and offices in heaped tiers of rubble, shattering windows a mile from ground zero. It killed sixty-three persons, thirty-nine inside the embassy compound, the rest passersby in cars or afoot. Eight of the seventeen dead Americans were CIA employees, including Robert Ames, Agency Station Chief Kenneth Haas, Near East Director Robert Ames, and most of the Beirut staffers. Also dead inside the embassy were William McIntire, deputy director of the U.S. Agency for International Development and two of his aides; two army sergeants and a marine corporal; an embassy guard; a journalist; thirty-two Lebanese clerical employees; and several of their countrymen waiting in line for visas to the States. Another 120 persons within range of the shrapnel and shockwave were injured.

And Devon, frankly, couldn't have cared less.

It was his brother's death that wounded him, compelling him to reevaluate the life Colby had picked to follow in their father's footsteps with the CIA, and Devon's decades with the FBI, also their dad's suggestion back in 1941, when the smoke was still rising from Pearl Harbor's wreckage.

What, if anything, had either one of them accomplished through those intervening years? Could it all, in fact, be summarized by Shakespeare's famed quotation from *Macbeth,* "a tale told by an idiot, full of sound and fury, signifying nothing"?

One thing Gantt knew, beyond a shadow of a doubt.

He couldn't meet that plane and watch the flag-draped caskets trundled out while Ron and Nancy Reagan grabbed their photo op for history.

To hell with that. Gantt had a better plan.

Reaching down to his hip, he lightly touched the Smith & Wesson Model 13 revolver holstered there, its cylinder loaded this morning with .357 Magnum rounds. Rising and straightening the papers on his desktop, he moved toward the men's room with determined strides.

Somebody else would have to bring him out.

———

HARLEM: October 7, 1983

NYPD SERGEANT PAYTON SAWYER found himself continually waiting for the other shoe to drop. No matter where he focused his attention lately, from the ghetto that had spawned him to the blighted, blasted slums of West Beirut, the forecast called for pain.

Drug use in Harlem, once his father's *bête noire*, was on the rise, both heroin and free-base crack cocaine. One thing that would've set his dad off was the fact that both drugs came into the country courtesy of U.S. agents using dope to fund illicit operations hidden by the all-inclusive veil of "national security." From what Payton had seen so far, feds weren't the only ones involved in trafficking. His own department skimmed its share of drug profits from syndicates peddling their shit, and sometimes served as escorts to whichever banks were laundering the dealers' loot this month.

Ironically, one of the few groups actively seeking to

purge narcotics from the ghetto was the newly formed Imam Al-Amin National Community—Al-Amin being the same radical jailbird formerly known as Rap Brown, paroled from Attica in 1976, lately returned from his tenure as a grocer in Georgia after cribbing guidelines from the Dar as-Salam ("House of Peace") movement down there. That struck Sawyer funny, coming from the same fire-breather who'd once said, "Violence is as American as cherry pie." Now Brown was following the road once trod by Malcolm X, trying to drive all Gotham's pimps and pushers out, sending them who knew where.

Some who still believed in revolutionary violence had met their match in court this year, convicted of participating in New Jersey's 1981 Brink's robbery and the associated murders, plus assorted other crimes. Kathy Boudin had pled guilty to one count each of felony murder and robbery, receiving a sentence of twenty years to life at New York's Bedford Hills Correctional Facility for Women. Her lover, David Gilbert, rolled the dice with a jury and stood convicted on three counts of felony murder, pulling seventy-five years to life while Weatherman Underground veterans William Ayres and Bernardine Dohrn adopted the son he'd fathered with Boudin.

Another loser in the trial sweepstales, Silvia Baraldini, had received a forty-three-year sentence: twenty years for joining in JoAnne Chesimard's prison break, twenty more for conspiring with the Black Liberation Army on two armed robberies, and three for criminal contempt of court. Assuming she lived to see parole, Washington and Rome's Ministry of Justice had made a deal for her repatriation to Italy, land of her birth. On the more merciful side, Amnesty International was on her case, laboring in tandem with the ACLU.

Brink's defendants Judith Clark and Donald Weems had been convicted with David Gilbert, choosing cohort Nathaniel Burns as their sole defense witness, ranting to the court that armed robbery was merely "expropriation" of money to bankroll a new revolutionary regime in America. Jurors couldn't swallow that, nor could Judge David Ritter, who handed them both seventy-five-year prison terms matching Gilbert's. Nat Burns, meanwhile, left court in chains to complete his own forty-year federal sentence.

And who won in the end?

The more he thought about it, Sawyer couldn't think of anyone at all.

———

FBI FIELD OFFICE, Manhattan: October 16, 1983

SPECIAL AGENT ERIN O'HARA finished reading the owner's manual for her new Motorola DynaTAC 8000X cellular telephone, still wondering if she'd made a foolish investment. It wasn't cheap or handy, for damned sure—$3,995 retail, thirteen inches long including its antenna, weighing one pound fifteen ounces, and it took ten hours to recharge—but it stored thirty phone numbers in its computerized memory. Service through an outfit called Ameritech cost another $50 per month, plus 40¢ per minute from 9 a.m. to 5 p.m., 24¢ off-peak, but she still had cash left over from one of her brother's life insurance policies, and what else did she plan to spend it on?

Why not a glimpse of the future?

Granted, she'd had to buy a larger handbag to accommodate the phone, but it also contained Bureau accessories including extra handcuffs, spare pistol ammunition, a spray can of Chemical Mace, and a Maglite that could double as a blackjack in a pinch. Those items, plus a travel pack of Kleeenex and some ChapStick ought to get her through the worst of duty days.

Not that she'd needed them so far, during her paper chase of rumored Soviet illegals in New York, but you could never tell. And if her nagging doubts about one of her own colleagues proved out...

She still had nothing she could put on paper with regard to Agent Stephen Barnes, and while he'd seemed more amiable toward her lately, Erin caught a whiff of overcompensation every time he smiled at her. Something was going on with him, but pinning down the *what* and *why* of it eluded her.

Meanwhile, she still kept track of the fallout from Operation ABSCAM, as the crooks impersonating public servants faced their days in court. Representative Frank Thompson had spent $24,000 of campaign funds fighting and appealing his criminal conviction—a new offense in itself—but time had finally run out and he'd begun to serve his three-year prison term for bribery.

Thompson had introduced another congressman, John Murphy, to the Bureau's bogus sheiks, and while he'd pocketed $50,000, a video glitch had prevented jurors from seeing the hand-off on tape, so his charge was reduced to "receiving an unlawful gratuity." His sentence: the same three years handed to Thompson.

South Carolina's John Jenrette got two years for his $50,000 payoff, caught on video telling an undercover G-man, "I've got larceny in my blood." From other remarks, it seemed he also liked banging his wife behind a column on the Capitol steps when House sessions ran into the night.

In March, dissatisfied with the Levi guidelines imposed on FBI sting operations before Ronald Reagan moved into the White House, Attorney General William Smith replaced them with his own set of rules, ostensibly trying to rescue First Amendment freedoms from Bureau headquarters. Meanwhile, "First Friend" Paul Laxalt, senator from Nevada, was nagging pal Reagan day and night to limit or totally terminate Bureau investigation of the Silver State's mobbed-up casino owners. On the side, he'd filed a libel suit against the Sacramento *Bee* newspaper for suggesting untaxed profits from the Ormsby House, a casino his family ran in Carson City during the 1970s.

Cause and effect?

On the side, Laxalt freely admitted long-running friendships with Cleveland mobster turned Vegas "godfather" Moe Dalitz and Teamster "consultant" Allen Dorman, stepson of Chicago labor racketeer Paul "Red" Dorfman. Back in 1974, Allen had been indicted over fraudulent Teamster loans, but the case fell through when a key prosecution witness was murdered. In December 1982 he'd been convicted on similar charges, resulting from the Bureau's "Operation Pendorf" (for "*pen*etration of *Dorf*man"), but he hadn't been sentenced when gunmen ventilated him outside an Illinois hotel.

Lie down with dogs, O'Hara thought.

And had to wonder once again who Stephen Barnes was playing footsie with, assuming there was anyone at all.

———

TEGUCIGALPA, Honduras: October 29, 1983

WHAT DID it say about his job, Hardy Gantt asked himself, if taking time off for the stateside double funeral of his father and uncle felt like a relief?

His dad, Colby, had gone down in the service of the Agency they'd both served, killed when Muslim terrorists bombed Beirut's U.S. Embassy in April. That had been a shock, but not entirely unexpected once the old man had received a parting field assignment to a war zone on the eve of his retirement.

Call it piss-poor luck, but that didn't account for Uncle Devon's suicide, committed in a bathroom at the Hoover Building on the very morning when his twin's corpse was returning from Beirut with other martyrs from the embassy.

What had gone through the aging G-man's mind before he locked himself inside that toilet stall, sat down, and used a Magnum round to paint the walls blood-red? Was he distraught over his brother's death? Doubting himself on other, unknown grounds? Or had he just turned yellow after all?

That didn't sound like Devon, who'd been kicking ass and taking names since World War Two, but when you got right down to it, who ever really knew another individual?

Who ever really knew *himself,* until the chips were down?

At least Honduras was a change of pace from counting bodies in El Salvador, if only as a matter of degree. The government's Special Investigations Branch had changed its name again, reverting to the original Intelligence

Battalion 3–16, its agents still using the same CIA torture manuals that had been its primers since General Policarpo García had deposed another military tyrant, General Juan Melgar Castro, back in 1978. The manuals taught a wide range of "coercive techniques," ranging from sensory deprivation and hypnosis to beatings and electric shocks, while warning anyone who cared that "the threat of pain is often more effective than the pain itself."

Of course, that hadn't stopped a series of assassinations and "disappearances," carried out with help from Chile's DINA, the Argentine Anticommunist Alliance, and quasi-freelance Argentine Colonel Mohamed Alí Seineldín, born Catholic in Uruguay but converted since then to become a Druze Muslim. Most Intelligence Battalion officers had graduated from the U.S. Army's School of the Americas and seemed to love applying what they'd learned there to Honduran fellow countrymen.

El Savador, meanwhile, was still the bloody stew that it had been when Hardy went home to grieve briefly with survivors of his shattered family. By May of this year, U.S. Army officers had assumed key positions in the Salvadoran military, flush with cash from the Reagan White House and Congress. Neutral observers claimed some 85 percent of civilian killings so far were committed by Salvadoran troops or death squads in league with President Álvaro Magaña's regime. The latest scorched-earth crackdown on dissent, begun in March, included the army kidnapping and fatal torture of Marianella García Villas, president of the Non-Governmental Human Rights Commission of El Salvador. President Reagan didn't seem to mind, and Langley wasn't bitching, as long as the war paid great dividend to its "black" budget.

Narcotics trafficking remained a staple of the Agency's

portfolio, the only way its leaders could conceive to fund a Contra war in Nicaragua that Congress had barred the U.S. from supporting. That meant undercutting anything the DEA might do to fight the Medellín Cartel, responsible for 240 political murders in Colombia so far this year alone. Victims ranged from two native cops who'd busted Pablo Escobar back in '76 to regional farmers, community leaders, and elected national officials.

A fair share of the drugs exported from South and Central America still made their way to Mena Intermountain Municipal Airport in Arkansas, widely recognized as an Agency drop point the same way certain Southeast Asian landing strips had been for Air America during the wars in Laos and Vietnam. If narco agents or nosy reporters caught the scent, it helped that former CIA director George H. W. Bush was now Vice President of the United States.

Some things would never change, Hardy supposed. Even when a surviving Paraguayan torture victim and a judge, José Fernández, uncovered their nation's classified "Archives of Terror" in Asunción, documenting 80,000 murders and imprisonment of 400,000 victims by Operation Condor spanning four nations, most of the "free world" refused to believe.

And why in hell should they, Hardy wondered, *when the crimes had been committed in their name?*

Now, the U.S. itself had invaded the tiny island nation of Grenada, ostensibly to "rescue" American students— working toward degrees from a last-ditch Third World medical school—from Prime Minister Maurice Bishop's Marxist-Leninist New Jewel Movement, established in 1979. Reagan dubbed the action "Operation Urgent Fury," a title owing more to his Hollywood B-movies than reality, but his constituents were in the mood to kick a little ass abroad, after the hostage crisis in Iran and bombings in Beirut.

The conquest only took four days, fielding Army Rangers and Delta Force, Navy SEALs and Marines against barely-trained Grenadan troops backed up by a handful of Cubans and Russians. Hardy had been pleased to miss it, while he kept up with the action via TV and agency memos.

Central America was bad enough to keep him occupied, at least till Langley changed its mind and shipped him somewhere else.

———

FBI FIELD OFFICE, Manhattan: November 24, 1983

AGENT STEPHEN BARNES wondered if he was turning paranoid. It was an occupational hazard for someone in his unique position—born in Moscow, son of a high-ranking KGB officer, smuggled into the States as a toddler and raised by Russian sleeper agents, groomed from birth for a single goal in life: to infiltrate the FBI and wreck it from within.

Was he imagining suspicion aimed his way by one inquisitive colleague, or had Erin O'Hara truly set her sights on him, while maintaining a cordial façade?

Barnes, as a dedicated Communist, despised religion, but a part of his American upbringing had included studying the so-called "Holy Bible" as a youth. Today, a verse from Proverbs Chapter 28 came back to him: "The wicked flee when no man pursueth; but the righteous are bold as a lion."

Which was he? Pursuing his late father's dream of vengeance, Barnes didn't regard himself as "wicked," necessarily, though most Americans—and everyone inside the Bureau—would condemn him as a traitor. Conversely, if his goal was "righteous" in the light of moral payback, then he should be bold, though not without the caution dictated by common sense.

As yet, he couldn't prove O'Hara had made any moves against him. Barnes was watchful, constantly on guard, particularly during mail drops and his periodic meetings with Lieutenant- Colonel Bobrik of the KGB. Certain that he had not been followed—or as certain as he could be, anyway—Barnes knew his office telephone might well be tapped without a warrant or involvement of technicians in the world beyond the Hoover Building.

That would be no problem, he'd decided, since his office calls were strictly Bureau business, and the few personal calls he made from home involved ordering takeout meals or chatting with a certain Brooklyn waitress he'd pretended to admire, thus keeping up his front as "one of the boys."

At work, he did what was expected of him, poring over files about the Soviet involvement in Afghanistan. That was a mess, as everyone on Earth must know by now, with Moscow seeking what Dick Nixon earlier had labeled "peace with honor," while the CIA kept arming mujahideen guerillas and sending them cash to continue their war of attrition. Otherwise, he scanned incoming tips and rumors for potential leads to Soviet illegals operating stateside, recognizing most such tales as total crap, cautioning Bobrik if it ever seemed that there might be a grain of truth involved.

At home, Yuri Andropov had suffered total kidney failure in February, entering Moscow's Central Clinical Hospital with no prospect of emerging alive. In September, Korean Air Lines Flight 007 had strayed over Russian soil due to a navigation error, and some military idiot had scrambled jets to shoot it down, killing all 269 persons aboard and provoking a humiliating international incident. In response, just yesterday, President Reagan had ordered deployment of U.S. cruise and Pershing II missiles in Western Europe.

Barnes worried about Reagan, questioning whether his starboard political tilt might brush against senility to end the world, but for now, the ex-actor seemed entranced by "Star Wars"—the Strategic Defence Initiative, conceived to develop a sophisticated anti-ballistic missile system of launching pads floating in space, to deter ICBM attacks upon America from other countries. The notion bore no signs of feasibility, and Barnes suspected it was just another scheme by Reagan's party to embezzle from the U.S. Treasury under the guise of national defense.

That, in itself, was fine with Barnes. But if the wild hare gave the slightest hint of being realized, he'd have to pass that on and let the chips fall where they might.

———

BIRMINGHAM, *Alabama: December 13, 1983*

TWELVE DAYS REMAINED UNTIL CHRISTMAS, and once again Dave Jordan wondered how he'd wound up spending nearly half his life below the Mason-Dixon Line. At first, he had been grateful to escape New York and all the bloody business that his family engaged in on a daily basis, leading to his father's death.

These days, it simply felt like home.

"Twelve days of Christmas start tomorrow," Fee O'Hara said, relaxing with a glass of wine at Jordan's side. "What are you getting me?"

"A history lesson," Dave said. "Did you know the twelve days actually *start* on Christmas Day and go on until January 6?"

"No presents, then?"

"The four weeks *prior* to Christmas are called Advent."

"I guess my gift will be solution of the Mobile lynching, then."

Dave knew Fiona had been disappointed when the FBI examined Michael Donald's death in 1981 and closed the case without discovering a federal crime they could hang charges on. Dissatisfied, Mobile's U.S. attorney had succeeded in reviving that inquiry, and the second time around, one of the murderers had cracked under interrogation. "Tiger" Knowles turned out to be a coward, swapping life in prison for his testimony against Henry Hays, and Jordan was surprised when jurors not only convicted Hays but fixed his penalty as death. If the state went through with it, Hays would be the first white man executed for killing an African American in Alabama since 1913, when two outlaws stretched rope for murdering a wealthy planter's black fighting cock trainer.

Governor Wallace had also been full of surprises this year, appointing two blacks to his cabinet and moving toward a record of black appointments overall. The Klan despised him, naturally, but for the first time since his famous loss in 1958, Wallace didn't appear to give a damn.

Could anybody change, given sufficient time? Dave wasn't sure, but he was old enough to wonder if the separation from his Gotham family and labors on behalf of Legal Aid entitled him to something like forgiveness when the final curtain fell.

If sins were passed down over generations, Jordan reckoned he was screwed.

———

FBI FIELD OFFICE, Manhattan: December 16, 1983

THE UNABOMBER SEEMED to be on holiday, no parcels mailed of detonated in seventeen months, and the task force was at loose ends, discarding its psychological profile and starting over from scratch.

That didn't bother Special Agent Wyman Gantt, since he'd inherited a slew of other bombing cases since his father's shocking suicide at Bureau headquarters in April. Glad for the distraction, he had thrown himself into pursuit of the United Freedom Front, always one step behind as its fugitive members stepped up their terror campaign.

The rash of bombings had begun on January 28th, when an explosion damaged Staten Island's federal building. Wyman was on bereavement leave for the next attack, on May 25th, when a ten-pound charge struck the National War College at Fort Lesley J. McNair, in Washington, D.C. An army spokesman tried to shrug it off, calling the damage superficial, "windows blown out, things of that nature."

On May 12th, anonymous calls to a crisis hotline and a doughnut shop warned of a time bomb ticking down at the Army Reserve Center in Uniondale, Long Island. Police rolled up just as the blast went off, causing extensive damage to the building. One day later, a similar bomb detonated in Queens, at the Naval Reserve Center, again without injuring anyone.

The bombers took a break then, returning on August 18th to blast a computer operations center at the Washington Navy Yard. Recorded phone messages to United Press International and the *Washington Post* claimed credit for Puerto Rico's FALN, buy Gantt smelled a rat, one batch of subversives trying to steal a competitor's thunder.

Three days later, a bomb caused major damage to a National Guard armory in the Bronx. That time, a UFF caller sent *New York Times* stringers scuttling to the site where a communiqué awaited them, condemning American militarism.

November's target was the U.S. Senate, nearly deserted at 10:58 p.m. on the 7th, when an explosion caused $250,000 damage. A follow-up call to the White House switchboard claimed credit for the UFF's "Armed Resistance Unit," blaming the attack on "American aggression" in Lebanon and Grenada. The caller had declared, "We purposely aimed our attack at the institutions of imperialist rule rather than at individual members of the ruling class and government. We did not choose to kill any of them this time. But their lives are not sacred."

At mid-morning on December 13th, a caller warned that three bombs were located in the Navy District Recruiting center in East Meadow, New York, set to blow in twenty minutes. Police found two briefcases thought-fully labeled "BOMB" and draped them with explosive blankets before they detonated at 11:48 a.m., but no third device was discovered.

Finally—at least, so far—UPI's Manhattan office received two late-night calls yesterday, warning that a pair of bombs were counting down at the Honeywell office in Queens. Police found the devices and removed them, with help from a Bureau explosives technician, and hauled them off to a bomb disposal site at Rodman's Neck in the Bronx. Examination showed that only one attaché case contained a bomb, quickly defused. The other held a UFF communiqué blaming the abortive attack on U.S. involvement in Central America.

And they weren't finished yet, Wyman guessed, surprised to notice that he didn't mind. Until the Unabomber finally emerged from hibernation—if he ever did—distraction was exactly what Gantt needed to prevent him dwelling on the evil fate that seemed to stalk his family.

A LOOK AT: BLOOD SPORT
(VICAP BOOK 1)

Los Angeles is city primeval, home base for the socio-pathic elite. Charles Manson. The Hillside Strangler. And now—the Reaper. He hunts at night terrorizing whole families at gunpoint, mutilating and finally slaughtering them. Dozens of victims. No survivors. No Clues.

Special Agents Joe Flynn and Martin Tanner, are highly trained members of the Federal Bureau of Investigation's Violent Criminal Apprehension Program. But the Reaper never leaves a trace. Flynn and Tanner can do nothing except pace in the shadows of the sleeping city waiting for the Reaper to strike again.

The case files of Special Agents Flynn and Tanner are a scorching record of brutal crime. Their Los Angeles is an urban nightmare ruled by psychotic lords of violence. But VICAP agents are tough and resourceful—and they never give up.

Though this series is fiction, VICAP is a real organization initially conceived in the late 1960s when the crimes of the Boston Strangler, Charles Manson, and other "motiveless" killers began to make national headlines.

A Look at: Blood Sport (VICAP Book 1)

AVAILABLE NOW

ABOUT THE AUTHOR

A California native, Michael Newton has published 215 books under his own name and various pseudonyms since 1977. He began writing professionally as a "ghost" for author Don Pendleton on the best-selling Executioner series and continues his work on that series today. With 104 episodes published to date, Newton has nearly tripled the number of Mack Bolan novels completed by creator Pendleton himself.

Newton's first book under his own name was *Monsters, Mysteries and Man* (1979), a survey of unexplained phenomena for younger readers. While 156 of Newton's published books have been novels—including westerns, political thrillers and psychological suspense—he is best known for nonfiction, primarily true crime and reference books.

www.ingramcontent.com/pod-product-compliance
Lightning Source LLC
Chambersburg PA
CBHW022145240626
47153CB00007B/2515